Tanka Soci

MW01602818

Foundeu in ∠000

Official Website: www.tankasocietyofamerica.org

Ribbons **Editor:** Christine L. Villa
5040 Jackson Street #86, North Highlands, CA 95660;
clvribbons@gmail.com

Book Review Editor: Tamara K. Walker
6127 W. Elmhurst Drive, Littleton, CO 80128; heliotropicink@gmail.com

Tanka Prose Editor: Susan Weaver
127 N. 10th Street, Allentown, PA 18102; tankaproseribbons@gmail.com

President: Michael Dylan Welch
22230 N.E. 28th Place, Sammamish, WA 98074-6408; welchm@aol.com

Vice President: Susan Burch
9128 Cool Hollow Terrace, Hagerstown, MD 21740;
sehbtree@yahoo.com

Secretary: Kath Abela Wilson
439 S. Catalina Avenue, #306, Pasadena, CA 91106;
poetsonsite@gmail.com

Treasurer: James Won
6233 Golden West, Temple City, CA 91780; jameswon@charter.net

Webperson: Michael Dylan Welch
22230 N.E. 28th Place, Sammamish, WA 98074-6408; welchm@aol.com

Layout: Taura Scott
512 E. Cherry Avenue, Monrovia, CA 91016, mewse@yahoo.com

Cover: *Cities at Dusk*. Watercolor on paper, 9 x 12, by Tiffany Shaw-Diaz. www.tiffanyshawdiaz.com

Cover Design: Kathleen Sue Mallari

Submission Guidelines: See last pages of journal.

Business Address: 439 S. Catalina Avenue, #306, Pasadena, CA 91106

Ribbons: **Tanka Society of America Journal**, a triannual publication appearing in Winter, Spring/Summer, and Fall. All prior copyrights are retained by contributors and full rights revert back on publication. Neither the Tanka Society of America, TSA officers, nor the *Ribbons* editor assume responsibility for views of any contributors (including TSA officers) whose work is printed in *Ribbons*.

TSA Memberships include three issues of the Tanka Society of America's journal, *Ribbons*. One-year membership in USD: $30 USA; $35 Canada and Mexico; $42 elsewhere. Make all checks or money orders payable to the Tanka Society of America and mail to Kath Abela Wilson, TSA Secretary, 439 S. Catalina Ave. #306, Pasadena, CA 91106.

Additional copies of recent issues of *Ribbons* may be ordered from our production partner at www.lulu.com. (Payment by PayPal is available from Lulu.) For questions about payment for non-US residents, contact Kath Abela Wilson by email: poetsonsite@gmail.com.

ISSN: 2150-4954

RIBBONS

Winter 2020: Volume 16, Number 1

CONTENTS

The Back Cover

coloring
inside the line
of a perfectly round moon
she remembers
her dead mother

Elisa Theriana

I selected this tanka because, despite its simplicity, it has a lot of dreaming room. From the first part of the tanka, we are able to conjure up the image of a child or an adult coloring inside the line of a perfectly round moon. Is she enjoying the moment? Is she pressured while coloring inside the line? The tanka shifts after the third line. What does she remember? I believe any reader will be intrigued at this point.

This tanka resonates with me because it reminds me of my mother, who passed away when I was eight years old. As a child, I grew up with strict rules and high expectations. My mother didn't accept anything that was average and, as a result, I was pressured to be perfect at everything I did. I perpetually lived in fear and caution. Even as I grew older, there were times when I still thought about disappointing my mother because of my life choices. For me, the perfectly round moon symbolizes the beliefs and standards my mother set and I am the child or the adult trying to please her.

When asked about her tanka, Elisa Theriana writes, "I lost my mom when I was 5. Long before that, my mother was ailing from cancer and I didn't really get the chance to know her. I keep the memory of her photograph in my mind. All the people who knew her told me how beautiful she was. She was a sweet and demure woman. So to me, she is 'a perfectly round moon.' 'Coloring inside the line' is about me trying to be like her."

It is apparent that the poet wrote this tanka from a different angle. She colors inside the line because she wants to be perfect like the "round moon," a metaphor for her dead mother. A reader may also conclude that this tanka is about not thinking outside the box. Some of us are restricted or discouraged from "coloring outside the line" because we are brought up to believe or accept only one way of doing or looking at things. This limited belief was either passed on to us by our parents or teachers or dictated to us by religion or tradition. I won't be surprised if another reader can unravel another layer of meaning to this tanka. The strength of this poem lies in its openness to more than one interpretation.

Editor's Message

I would like to, first and foremost, extend my gratitude to David Rice for entrusting me with the editorship of *Ribbons*. I am deeply honored to have been given this opportunity to serve the tanka community. At the same time, it is also humbling knowing that I have big shoes to fill and a lot more to learn as the new editor of this prestigious journal.

I am sure most of you are curious to know about my preferences while reviewing submissions and what kind of work compels me to send out an acceptance letter. I would like to take this opportunity to shed more light on this. At first glance, I do not favor lengthy lines in tanka. Each word should count and I do not advocate padding. I gravitate toward concrete imagery. Does the poet use fresh metaphors? Does the poem *show* me something as opposed to merely stating it? The way a tanka sounds is also essential. Is it lyrical? Do the words flow naturally? Does the tanka have a strong juxtaposition? Is it linear or does it have a pivot? I look for that something extra or an element of surprise. These are some of the characteristics of a good tanka that move me in some way. The key element, though, is the amount of dreaming room a tanka lends itself to. If I can go back to reading the tanka and unpeel another layer of meaning, then it has ample ambiguity to create depth. It may be difficult to find all of these in a single tanka as I plough through submissions, but these are my guidelines as both a poet and an editor.

I look forward to your submissions. I hope you take this time to read and write more tanka as we face the challenges of this current pandemic.

Stay healthy and safe!

Thank you!

—Christine L. Villa

scratching
my winter funk
into a turtle
with each stroke
the blues disappear

tanka by Pamela A. Babusci
artwork by Christine L. Villa

The Tanka Café

Featured at the Café

With each issue, a "Member's Choice Tanka" will be selected from the previous installment of the "Tanka Café" to receive an honorarium of $25. Monies for the award are provided from the general fund of the Tanka Society of America. All poems appearing in each installment of the "Tanka Café" will be eligible for this recognition.

Each recipient of the "Member's Choice Tanka" award is asked to make the next award selection along with two or three commended poems from the subsequent set, and to offer a few comments regarding their choice for the award. In the present case, Michele H. Harvey has chosen our "Member's Choice Tanka" and commended poems from the "Time" set appearing in the Fall 2019 installment of the "Tanka Café."

—Michael McClintock

Member's Choice Tanka
Michele L. Harvey

My grateful thanks to Jenny Ward Angyal for her kindness in choosing my What Matters poem from the last Tanka Café. There is nothing more gratifying in life than the gift of being understood. I thank her too, for her sensitive assessment.

As always, Michael McClintock has tasked us once again, with an admirable theme. In his introduction to the subject, he talks about Stephen Hawking's idea of time as a "function of consciousness" or mind. If time is a construct created by mind, a fixed point is needed to orient to, to make it functional. As I strolled through the open doors and wondrous worlds of the ninety-eight poems accepted on the subject, I was struck by how each poem is revelatory, in accord with its own fixed point: the poet. What I cherish in poetry, above all else, is the presentation of a larger viewpoint (its revelation,) which in turn reveals my own limitation. It may suddenly take me out of my clam-like existence, leaving me blinking on a strange shore. Or it may dazzle me with unimagined word pairings and images. At every instance a great poem makes me forget myself and my world, transporting me to the unknown.

With the capacious theme of time, I originally looked only toward the grand definition, but my fellow poets quickly reminded me that time can be cut down to a single, fixed moment, from which all else springs. In that one defining moment, a poet puts me in his or her shoes.

One such poem which presented this forceful winnowing was Susan Constable's (my Member's Choice pick.) Here she revisits what must be the defining moment in her life, which altered it forever. The cruel beauty with which she describes time as "an elastic band," depicts the warping and constricting quality such a moment creates. Once experienced, it can never be escaped.

the pull of time
like an elastic band . . .
a sudden death
stretching a moment
into forever

Susan Constable

The following honorable mention poems I list below in no special order.

The poem by Maryalicia Post also adds a warning, akin to George Santayana's quote, "Those who cannot remember the past are condemned to repeat it." I do not know what wounds lay beneath her "crust of days," but I do know I shouldn't like them to awaken.

> time heals—
> a fragile scab will form
> take care
> beneath a crust of days
> old wounds remain

> *Maryalicia Post*

Robert Kusch gives us poem which describes how some things can haunt us even when we don't initially understand why, which step out of the time's shadow later on.

> so many years
> it meant nothing to me
> that sign
> on the Outer Banks
> *a lighthouse once stood here*

> *Robert Kusch*

The last poem that I'll mention is James Chessing's, which very much reminded me of what my husband always says, that he "sees in me the girl he first met, no matter how long we're together." This at first seems too glib and smooth, but its simplicity in no way lessens the truth of it. We all have that self inside which transcends time, and those who love us the longest will always see it.

if I could smooth
the wrinkles from your face,
to see you once more,
all arms and legs, as the day
you ran my frisbee down

James Chessing

I heartily thank all the poets for opening their generous hearts in their offerings.

As always, it was an honor and great pleasure to read each and every one of your poems.

Tanka Café: Open Theme

In this open theme set, we have the privilege of looking over one another's shoulder to experience a moment or two magically inside the box of someone else's mind.

Of course, how fully we enter that place depends on the language used, the words chosen and how they are arranged. In tanka, as with any poetry, language does the heavy lifting. Tanka's specialized use of suggestion, ambiguity and nuance, association and allusion — which are fulcrums of the genre and its distinctive form — nudge a poem's language well beyond the purely literal, acting as portals for the reader to enter into the experience and supply details of contour, color and emotion that are, in fact, their own — from the reader's specific, private experience or memory.

A successful poem will create that fusion of poet-poem-reader for the most people, most of the time, and will be something that is tangible to thought and sense. Because of wide divergence in human experience, many poems will be closed doors to one reader and a vast, peopled and intricate field or space to another. Both readers engage the same poem, but what each takes away from the poem can be quite different in both effect and value as a piece of literature.

Another way to understand this is to think of the tanka as a kind of small, open stage that invites each member of the audience to walk on and play a role within the setting furnished by the playwright.

Given recent headlines and events in the world, who cannot contribute his or her detail to LeRoy Gorman's poem —

> horseshit
> where there are
> no horses
> anything's possible
> in politics

Among tanka poets, Gorman has a long-established reputation for caustic satire, summary of human foible, and blunt expression of thoughts that often sound like something we might have said but left unspoken. Gorman confesses, "I'm not sure if this poem suits but since it's an open theme I've chosen 'politics'. It's a theme I keep returning to even after I think I'm done with it."

And who, finding much to sympathize with in Gorman's poem, may not find themselves ready to search out personal meaning in John Tehan's tanka at the other end of the spectrum? —

> all things old
> made new again
> Dick and Jane redux
> frolic hand in hand
> down Memory Lane

John Tehan sends along these comments with his poem, referencing *The New Testament*: "Revelation 21:5 ('*Behold, I make all things new*') has always been one of my favorite Bible verses. It's been coming to mind frequently, lately, as I help my elderly sister adjust to living in a nursing home. There's a reminiscence group there they call 'Memory Lane' and I participate when I can. I find it fascinating to hear what the folks have remembered, rightly or wrongly, and what they've forgotten. Looking at them now, I imagine them many years and decades younger, living their lives in a kinder world, in gentler times, and I can't help but feel nostalgic for days gone by. Closing out this year, and preparing to welcome the next, brings sadness and joy in equal measure."

Claire Everett also was especially moved by the time of year when sending her poem. "Well, here I am again," she writes, "last minute, and it seems between decades, between worlds . . . spending my time supporting adults with learning disabilities, autism and complex needs, in this season when the world seems to stand still and spin out of control all at once, I have had little time to write or even ponder. But this [my poem] came on the walk to work this New Year's Eve."

To which thought Marje A. Dyck chimes in, "The years go by, and one realizes they will never be a Shakespeare, but in the simple pleasure of putting words together, it is always an adventure toward possibility! Keeping a sense of humour helps."

Carole Harrison speaks of what the world has heard much about. "Horrible time here in southern Australia," she tells us. "Although the closest fires are 30-40 km away from us, we have had thick grey smoke and red dust blanketing the sky and keeping us indoors with all windows firmly closed. Mother nature is speaking. . . Still, life goes on." Another Australian, Beatrice Yell, adds, "Along with bushfires, we have been experiencing gale-force wind gusts which have the entire east coast of Australia in a state of alarm. Trees and huge branches have come down to block highways and bring down power lines."

Picking up on the idea of making your open theme poem your last, Susan Burch sends this note—"I debated over sending this one because I liked it so much, but it seemed to perfectly fit the theme—the way I would want people to remember me. Even though I have an angry tanka book out, I want to think that people would see me as more than that, as a person who just wants to belong and be a loving part of this world." Another poet, Victor Ortiz, writes "For this open theme tanka, I've embraced the suggestion that I imagine that this is the last poem I'll ever write. This tanka, inspired by N. Scott Momaday, illustrates how I feel about being alive and where I feel most at home—when I'm in the desert."

Our correspondent in France, Giselle Maya, is one of those who went down Memory Lane, and what a memory it is she writes about. "Your 'open theme' awakened in me a long-ago adventure I had. I sailed with a four-woman crew and the captain/owner of the ship, a 45-foot ketch named *Neophyte*, from Sausalito to Hawaii in 1962-3. I had the opportunity to write about this in the *Honolulu Star Bulletin*, the *San Francisco Chronicle*, the magazine *Sailing,* and other journals. My son, who lives in Montrose, California, recently sent me a DVD of the film 'Maiden' about the racing yacht by that name. This awakened many memories of my own earlier voyage. I began writing tanka, connecting that adventure in sailing to writing . . . I am sending you one of the tanka I produced."

Autumn Noelle Hall explains how she went about responding to our theme. "My goodness, this Open theme of yours was SOOOOOO much harder than the usual assigned prompts! All that unrestricted freedom—I'm like a puppy at the dog park, dashing hither and thither, following this scent trail and that, leaping before I look. I finally decided that, rather than barking my fool head off about hard-hitting issues, I'd simply share my very best Christmas news. An unexpected opportunity to rescue a vision-impaired Aussie puppy opened me to possibilities I hadn't even considered. That opening, which is exactly what I needed most, seemed to fit your theme better than any other. . . I've included a couple pictures below my tanka, just so you can share in my joy. Her name is Holly, and we're bringing her home Christmas Eve."

Thanks for the photos, Autumn, but our readers will have to imagine what your new dog looks like from your poem alone.

Mark Teaford's comment applies well, I think, to Autumn's deed of rescue. We all have the potential to add immeasurably to other lives. We just need the vision and wisdom to do so."

We will close with these thoughts from Joy McCall. "Symbols have power," she begins. "Like the cross. And like the strange image of a woman which sits up under the eaves of an old church near our home. It's a church which was built on a bronze age burial mound, as so many were, the new religions trying to cover up the old ways. There are many bones of heathen chieftains that lie under Christian altars. I think those things have shaped and opened my own soul in some way. . . The *sheela-na-gig* has many origins and stories around her. She was first the protector of the home, her lifted skirts warding off evil spirits; the symbolic doorway where life begins. She was and is the witch, the hag, the crone, the goddess of the earth, the old woman, the matriarch of families. . . Now the generations before me have all passed away, the symbol means more to me. I am the oldest of my tribe. It all helps me to settle my mind with death and life and the dance between the two. The endless circling of time."

—*Michael McClintock*

an open mind
does not hold onto habits
like an old cloak
even my best-loved sweater
is full of moth holes

Neal Whitman, Pacific Grove, CA

this sudden urge
to clean the windows
inviting
the outside world
to add colour to my life

Keitha Keyes, Sydney, NSW, Australia

storming in the door
the boulder that the waves
beat their heads against
until they die
fell eons ago

James Chessing, San Ramon, CA

my new sofa
takes my breath away
nobody
bothered to tell me
formaldehyde comes free

Mary Davila, Buffalo, NY

Dad helps me up
into the Case tractor seat
he administers
my first driving lesson
too young to be of much help

Judith Morrison Schallberger, San Jose, CA

I lay down
in the borders
where blossoms fall
listening to a song
for the lost poet

Joanna Ashwell, Barnard Castle, UK

where the creek
becomes deep and still
sunlight glistens
off the parts of you
still undressed and wet

Bryan Rickert, Belleville, IL

at the museum
treasures of Troy . . .
glimpses
beneath glass
of life in another time

*Marilyn Humbert, Berowra Heights,
NSW, Australia*

my mom
ties my long hair
in a tight ponytail
one day I will decide
for myself

Christine L. Villa, North Highlands, CA

under the stars
everything is possible;
when clouds hide their light
darkness closes in,
faith extinguished

Edward J. Rielly, Westbrook, ME

quiet day . . .
along a country road
nothing but fragrance
and the humming of bees
in a hedge of lilacs

Elinor Pihl Huggett, Lakeville, IN

my wayward son
again asks for money
for the family
his kids are at risk
as is their Grandpa

Robert B McNeill, Winchester, VA

the sum of a life
is simply what can be
remembered
which like everything else
dissipates over time

Michael H. Lester, Los Angeles, CA

if I spin a globe
stop it with my finger
chances are
people are protesting
right there, in the street

Sally Biggar, Topsham, ME

that small cousin,
cowboy to my indian,
sharing birthdays
now toasts our seventy-eighth
in vintage champagne

Amelia Fielden, Belconnen, ACT, Australia

lost in diagnosis
defined by words
I can't pronounce
say my name
find me

Patricia Pella, Bristol, RI

winter sunlight
traversing row after row
of gravestones
a one-armed man speaks
to someone I cannot see

Chen-ou Liu, Ajax, ON, Canada

eons before
you were born
even then
I chose you
to be my mother

Marilyn Fleming, Pewaukee, WI

wounded
in body and mind
the exile
returns to a house
full of angry strangers

Ruth Holzer, Herndon, VA

frosty roofs
pale the autumn hues
I contemplate
my last chapter
under a cloudy sky

Nu Quang, Seattle, WA

I pass below
where she sits high and rude
under the sacred eaves
and I smile and bow my head
to sheela-na-gig

Joy McCall, Norwich, England

        sixty years
        pushed into the past
        a thick beige book
        full of tales and adventures
        as I move on . . . alone

        Kirsty Karkow, Blomstereng, Waldoboro, ME

I'm stuck on replay
and add one more smoking nail
to burn up my life
     once my strength as he lost his
        I'm no longer in control

Adelaide B. Shaw, Millbrook, NY

        clearing moon
        I look past the grey hair
        and rounded shoulders,
        treasure your kind eyes
        and laugh wrinkles

        Dawn Bruce, St Leonards, NSW, Australia

hesitant
inside the dance
my hands
embrace the space
between moving bodies

Gerry Jacobson, Canberra, Australia

skipping
the poetry class
for no reason
I have gifted
this day to myself

Ken Slaughter, Worcester, MA

foggy road
wild sunflowers
guide
my mind
toward light

Margarita Engle, Clovis, CA

a heavy weight
among three generations
was bitterness
learning to let go
brings peace

Carmen Sterba, University Place, WA

the best days
of our lives
begin with sunrise
. . . then we start
to make choices

Mark Teaford, Napa, CA

my life is open theme
the choice of path seems mine
but every day
unexpected twists and turns
transform its focus

Elaine Riddell, Hamilton, New Zealand

I am fragile
vulnerable like cellophane
yet hard to break
imbued with a certain strength
cursed with utter transparency

Carol Raisfeld, Atlantic Beach, NY

blank page
pen
thoughts
tea
blank page

P.O. Fieweger, West Bend, WI

too dark
to watch the evening wind
teasing the garden
childless, we contemplate
growing old together

Maxianne Berger, Montreal, QC, Canada

2020 vision—
we adopt a blind puppy
sensing the way
she'll train us to see
with our hearts

Autumn Noelle Hall, Green Mountain Falls, CO

crying door
everyone comes
into the bar
with their own sorrow . . .
happy hour

Mariko Kitakubo, Tokyo, Japan

the encumbered heart
and the jam-packed suitcase
never beyond capacity
always accommodate
one more

Margaret Van Every, Ajijic, Jalisco, Mexico

told she's wandering
granny stops
telling her story,
then says, I reckon
it's all connected

John Quinnett, Bryson City, NC

tangled
with a cricket's song
your name
the remnants of starlight
that outlives its nova sun

Kat Lehmann, Guilford, CT

I am the flash flood
I am the humming of bees
I am the taste of peyote
revealing illness . . .
yipping coyotes at dawn

Victor Ortiz, Bellingham, WA

on the Bay of Fundy
waking up to mudflats
and shells—morning is in
the swoop of a gull,
its skirring, its cries

Robert Kusch, Piscataway, NJ

opening out
into another dimension
the road ahead
transformed by snow, leads me
to question my life path

Susan Mary Wade, Littlehampton, West Sussex, UK

that long estrangement
never talked about
softening pears
we know only now
is relevant

Joyce Futa, Altadena, CA

Greenland
walking on a glacier
history
    melting
    under my feet

Robert Erlandson, Birmingham, MI

take the albatross
how did that word evolve
how did that elegant bird
become linked
to that elusive word

Giselle Maya, St. Martin de Castillon, France

who can tell
but if I keep
writing these poems
perhaps
an "oak-cleaving thunderbolt!"

Marje A. Dyck, Saskatoon, SK, Canada

forms in the mist
as if otherworldly . . .
in the moonlight
i watch the river
take on new life

Pat Geyer, East Brunswick, NJ

snow melt
how soon our seasons feed
the bubbling stream
I still see you bending down
to drink its water

Xenia Tran, Nairn, Scotland

doctor's office
we discuss the future
who will be around
to wipe
my drool

Dave Bachelor, Chicago, IL

Monday morning
don't want to get out
of my warm bed
keep the dreams rolling
while I lie undercover

Genie Nakano, Hawthorne, CA

snowflakes dance
outside an open window
still warm
the cushioned seat
on her walking frame

Hazel Hall, Aranda, ACT, Australia

a bottle
of some antiquity
beached
inside a note from me
"if you are called you must obey!"

Ken Anderson, Mornington, VIC, Australia

romantic evening
in a boutique hotel
a dream come true
but for all the pillows
that came between us

Bob Lucky, Jubail, Saudi Arabia

panic
where is inspiration
blank page
I've become dependent
upon suggestion

Ignatius Fay, Sudbury, ON, Canada

unfathomable
the winter sky
from my balcony
I still hear mother's voice
exhorting me to reach for the stars

Madhuri Pillai, Melbourne, Australia

high tide
takes away
their last breaths
  oh, but the weight of
  God's silence

(after 'Silence' [2016], director: Martin Scorsese)

Iliyana Stoyanova, St Albans, UK

open house
one by one the footsteps
fade away
how odd it is to have strangers
refurbish our dreams

Barun Saha, Bangalore, Karnataka, India

I descend
into the well
of myself . . .
home glimmers
like starlight

Dru Philippou, Taos, NM

beginning
a new phase of life
retirement village
old enough now to know
courage is my best friend

Catherine Smith, Sydney, NSW, Australia

the soft squeeze
of the child's hand . . .
a parade
passing by
and we're part of it

Rebecca Drouilhet, Picayune, MS

on her pallet
she is cold, hungry, alone
her mother gone into the night
      seeking
warmth, sustenance, companionship

Elizabeth Howard, Arlington, TN

shady morning lake
keeps time against the boat
damselfly
on my knee
sharing its metallic blue silence

Susan Weaver, Allentown, PA

puzzle books
her one indulgence—
she doesn't mind
when I solve a puzzle
mother loves me, too

Joyce S. Greene, Poughkeepsie, NY

strands
of pale seaweed
strewn
on driftwood—
this wayward life

Susan Constable, Parksville, BC, Canada

snowflakes
fill the sky at dawn
If only I could go skiing
during Christmas Holidays
as I did in my youth

Aya Yuhki, Tokyo, Japan

while writing checks
on the last day of the year
I say farewell
to regrets and sorrows
in the Year of the Boar

Margaret Chula, Portland, OR

drops of ink
fall on a blank page—
crows
on the winter wind
signifying nothing

Jenny Ward Angyal, Gibsonville, NC

my local universe
is big and busy enough
for me
no need to leave
the hundred aker wood

Charles Harmon, Los Angeles, CA

secure nest
of my childhood
when dad left
the bottom fell out
my mind opened

Kath Abela Wilson, Pasadena, CA

firstborn
gives his hand-me-downs
to last little brother
eagerly waiting for the baseball cap
and team uniform

Sharon Lynne Yee, Torrance, CA

after the storm
no power in the street
a single candle
takes us
into the shadows

Beatrice Yell, Belrose, Sydney, Australia

imagining
this wall pattern
(• • • – – – • • •)
distress signal
on the border

Don Miller, Las Cruces, NM

my door opens
on a new moon world
of frost and stars . . .
and a blackbird,
brighter still

*Claire Everett, Northallerton,
North Yorkshire, England*

an oak seedling rises
from a gnawed ribcage . . .
I don't want my body
to shrivel in a box
or blow away in the wind

Seren Fargo, Bellingham, WA

the deer eats
wildflowers I've come to see
she looks at me
across my lost landscape
and fills it with her eyes

Jeanne Cook, South Bend, IN

lulled by the train
friends' addresses tucked away
Disneyland beckons
through fields and prairies
to my new Golden State home

Patricia Wakimoto, Gardena, CA

doctor's office lobby
a panel of windows
in view of mountains
under a clear blue sky
here now, why wait

James Won, Temple City, CA

gifts under the tree
alive with the possibility
of anything and everything—
do we really
have to open them?

Elizabeth Martens, Philadelphia, PA

all things old
made new again
Dick and Jane redux
frolic hand in hand
down Memory Lane

John Tehan, Cape Cod, MA

sparks
shoot skywards—
she burns
a lot more
than memories tonight

Carole Harrison, Jamberoo, NSW, Australia

horseshit
where there are
no horses
anything's possible
in politics

LeRoy Gorman, Napanee, ON, Canada

The gap
in the dark enso
on pale paper
this first morning
of the rest of my life

J. Zimmerman, Santa Cruz, CA

what
lifetime achievement
need I have
except to love
and be loved

Susan Burch, Hagerstown, MD

bits and pieces
of my own self-deluding
a lifetime's work
dismantled in an instant
when going through death's door

Michele L. Harvey, Hamilton, NY

balanced stones
describe life's journey
a fragile dance
entwined branches
act as safety net

Joan E. Stern, Malibu, CA

Next Tanka Café Theme: Curiosity

Deadline: April 30th, 2020

The Tanka Society of America invites members to submit one original, unpublished tanka for each installment of "The Tanka Café" appearing in this journal.

Did curiosity really kill the cat? Write a tanka about experiencing a reward (or unwelcome result) arising from curiosity, or about an incident that awakened a desire to go sleuthing for more information and better understanding. Can you elevate your poem to achieve fresh insight into human nature or the human condition? Inquiring minds want to know. Serious or humorous treatments will be welcome.

Please note that poems submitted to Tanka Café are considered "published" when they appear; you therefore need to be cautious about submitting them to other venues, especially to contests, which may require that all work submitted be unpublished and/or not under consideration elsewhere. Generally, restrictions will be few and almost any treatment will be acceptable. The overall challenge will be to submit one's very best effort. All poems will be read for depth and "layering" of meaning, substance, thematic content, etc.

About eighty of the best poems fitting the theme will appear in the next installment of the Tanka Café. Please understand that any note accompanying your submission may also be considered for publication, in whole or in part. Send your submission to Michael McClintock via email to mchlmcclintock@aol.com with the subject heading "Tanka Café" (be certain to use the subject heading, please), or via mail to Michael McClintock, 1830 N. Bush Avenue, Clovis, CA 93619 (no SASE necessary). Be sure to include your full name as you wish it to appear beneath the poem, followed by your town or city of residence and its location (state, province, and country): see examples throughout this journal. Make sure this information appears in your submission—the best place to put it is beneath your poem, under your name. The in-hand deadline is April 30, 2020.

—Michael McClintock

Selected Tanka

nesting
of the night ravens
the rustle
of morning colors
like the lifting of wings

Kat Lehmann, Guilford, CT

rush of spring gusts
through the trees
on a long, empty afternoon . . .
I am a child again
walking the coastline

Anne Curran, Hamilton, New Zealand

the floorplan
of my childhood home
drawn from memory
a window opens
to the scent of lilacs

Jenny Ward Angyal, Gibsonville, NC

sunny yellow
raises the day . . .
as if
high flying
i am home free

Pat Geyer, East Brunswick, NJ

the smell
of freshly mown grass
summer in winter
as I walk barefoot
healing with each step

Genie Nakano, Gardena, CA

Sun-kissed clouds
skim the sky
erasing shadows
from the grass
where we were sweet and green

Jane Stuart, Greenup, KY

bluebird
fluffed in a sunray
let me cradle you
against my aged breast
an oven of warmth

Elizabeth Howard, Arlington, TN

this morning
while I wait on hold
my blood boiling
a rosebud blossoms
and a robin builds a nest

Michael H. Lester, Los Angeles, CA

on bin night
a walk to the kerb
under a veiled moon
the aroma of spring blooms
and newly-mown grass

Beatrice Yell, Belrose, Sydney, Australia

oranges on my tree
become silver globes
enchanted
I let the moon
gild me

Joyce Futa, Altadena, CA

firefly lights
along the road's edge
—how easily
a hundred little twinkles
change everything

Michael Blaine, Seaford, DE

a skydance
of winter sparrows
in dim light
this urge to dream
a different dream

Chen-ou Liu, Ajax, ON, Canada

revisions
one poem at a time
like days
on a calendar
leading toward spring

Margarita Engle, Clovis, CA

maw of the river
clinging to a branch
that moment
when I could have
changed my course

Marilyn Fleming, Pewaukee, WI

at my back
cold autumn wind
pushing me home
this damned decision
I've been avoiding

Ignatius Fay, Sudbury, ON, Canada

backing out
I try not to damage
anyone's car . . .
in a tight spot
between two friends

Ken Slaughter, Worcester, MA

I am cursed
to have too many rooms
not one feels like home—
on my screened porch
nature comforts me

David F. Noble, Charlottesville, VA

another summit
with a few wind-blown clouds—
the same emptiness
between you and the world
happens to be below

Mike Dillon, Puget Sound, WA

no one curled up
on his favorite chair—
with four cats remaining
how can a house
feel so empty?

Susan Weaver, Allentown, PA

during a winter freeze
the heartbeat of my life
craves hibernation
barren places
hold no comfort

Janet Qually, Memphis, TN

the rumoured coyote's
paw tracks in the snow
by the subway grate
I too feel out of place
and drawn to warmth

J. Brian Robertson, Toronto, Canada

surrounding myself
with comfort food
(whole wheat crackers
and peanut butter)
I reach for a knife

Don Miller, Las Cruces, NM

after the solstice
the light expands more
every day
i listen to my breath
joined to the here and now

Pasquale Asprea, Genoa, Italy

we follow
the call of tundra swans . . .
finding
beyond the neon lights
the pulse of home

Louisa Howerow, London, Canada

walking into fog
on the Maine coast
I wonder who it is—
this stranger
called myself

Robert Kusch, Piscataway, NJ

absence and yearning
nowhere to be reached—
white veils of waterfall
in the deep forest
begin to hide myself

Aya Yuhki, Tokyo, Japan

I suffer from
the impostor complex—
how can I call myself
a musician if I practice
the same partita 50 years?

Margaret Van Every, Ajijic, Jalisco, MX

as if
no cruelty had scathed me
I lie
in the softness of new snow
waving my arms into wings

Michele L. Harvey, Hamilton, NY

a wind song
in the sky
above the Roman ruins—
am I the trembling rose
pale pale purple?

Mariko Kitakubo, Tokyo, Japan

your face
in the telling . . .
how many clouds
can the sky hold
and not rain?

James Chessing, San Ramon, CA

new love
for paper plates
mother says
it has nothing to do
with this unending winter

Opeyemi P. Babafemi, Iloren, Nigeria

slow
moving traffic
the slip and slide
on a road of snow
and black ice

James Won, Temple City, CA

in spite of
climate change
babies
insist on being born—
salmon struggling upstream

Sheila Sondik, Bellingham, WA

bushfire smoke
worms its way into our house
and worried minds
high up, storm clouds
slink away in silence

Sandra Renew, Canberra, Australia

a bitter taste
to end-of-year coffee—
conversations turn to
trauma in our own backyard
and around the globe

Elaine Riddell, Hamilton, New Zealand

there is much ado
about the latest
celebrity scandal
the ocean swells
the ocean recedes

LeRoy Gorman, Napanee, ON, Canada

panoramic view
from my high rise apartment
a man far below
in a tiny garden
never looks up

Bob Lucky, Jubail, Saudi Arabia

a sagging gate
grates across the walk
difficult to open
people's minds are often
tilted to one end

James B. Peters, Cottontown, TN

black and white
this sweep of checkered tile
in the abbey's quire
I contemplate a world
where answers are clear-cut

Janet Lynn Davis, Grimes County, TX

at interfaith group,
the girl lets my daughter peek
under her hijab . . .
our similarities
so often hidden from view

Grix, Wilmington, DE

gathered around
the table, we watch uncle
carve the turkey
a Norman Rockwell picture
on the wall

Claire Vogel Camargo, Austin, TX

under the arbor
rose hips buffeted
by a winter gust
the scent
of your skin

Michael D. Mann, Shallotte, NC

shadows
brightened by waves . . .
as the water recedes
your words gentle
my soul

Marje A. Dyck, Saskatoon, SK, Canada

deep at night
the moon on snowy windows
sparkles, sparkles
the light always returns
your smile behind the lens

Xenia Tran, Nairn, Scotland

for a week
his soup pot wafting
you'll get well
after thirty years
the broth still simmers

Mira Walker, Canberra, Australia

the bind
of my wedding vows
untethered
a work horse
becomes a brumby

Liz Lanigan, Canberra, Australia

autumn mountains
reverberate with
a magpie's song
will we ever get
tired of each other?

Hemapriya Chellappan, Chennai, India

centering
clay on a wheel
I think of us
and what we might
have become

Bryan Rickert, Belleville, IL

impatient,
I await her
response to my text . . .
a fly hovers over
the fruit bowl

David Read, Calgary, Alberta, Canada

rinsing rice
in the cloudy water
a vision
of this mute phone
remaining mute

Barun Saha, Bangalore, India

now, in the afternoon
rain clouds have cleared
but in the morning
when you hadn't yet called
the sky fell dark upon my cheeks

Michael Dylan Welch, Sammamish, WA

the blackbird's song
more ominous
now
his silent treatment
nothing new to me

Jackie Chou, Pico Rivera, CA

thinking
today will be different
I reach for her
. . . ice bridge
over a river

Mark Teaford, Napa, CA

between bites
of her toast
the latest appeal
that we pick up
and move . . .

Tom Clausen, Ithaca, NY

a friend tells me
she's getting divorced . . .
holes in the earth
where sunflower seeds
had been

Jennifer Hambrick, Columbus, OH

and so
our poetry is of partings
even as we meet . . .
a glass tassel of dew
dissolves in the sun glow

Sonam Chhoki, Thimphu, Bhutan

green, green, green!
the song of the treetop thrush
today I feel my age
in my heart
not my bones

Claire Everett, Northallerton, North Yorkshire, England

on a tranquil evening
crimson and gold leaves
float down . . .
how beautiful
to age gracefully

Catherine Smith, Sydney, NSW, Australia

how shrunken
that childhood house becomes
as I age
my dwelling place grows
larger and larger

Jeanne Cook, South Bend, IN

becoming
more inflexible
with the passing years
even the air mattress
has taken on my shape

Seren Fargo, Bellingham, WA

how the years
gather speed—
I remember
a flash of golden wings
beside the morning train

Carole Harrison, Jamberoo, NSW, Australia

tripping over
the debris of autumn—
what doesn't
kill me outright
will in a little while

Ruth Holzer, Herndon, VA

the underside
of the carriage—
the days
I can barely
function

Susan Burch, Hagerstown, MD

dark marks
on paper
old eyes
struggle to harvest
a poem

Dave Bachelor, Albuquerque, NM

a hamster
keeps running
on his wheel . . .
everything I did today
I'll do again tomorrow

Susan Constable, Parksville, BC, Canada

whispers
of winter wind
through every crack . . .
she tells me a secret
I already know

Dawn Bruce, St. Leonards, NSW, Australia

memory rings
of a giant redwood
my fingers
stroll between
two worlds

Dru Philippou, Taos, NM

She veers wildly
backing down the driveway
peering in mirrors—
the growing aroma
of crushed lavender

J. Zimmerman, Santa Cruz, CA

last rays
of the day's light
blinding
you refuse to see clearly
how this addiction changed you

Marjorie Buettner, Chisago City, MN

where are the robins
harbingers of spring?
no sign
of anything
before the diagnosis

Maxianne Berger, Montreal, QC, Canada

in the night
the cold shivering cry
of a screech owl . . .
has death come for you
at last, old friend?

John Quinnett, Bryson City, NC

drip drip
of my teabag
two deaths
too many
this past year

Louise Dandeneau, Winnipeg, MB, Canada

i wrap
fewer Christmas gifts
this season
the first bittersweet sip
of a "Compari"

Judith Morrison Schallberger, San Jose, CA

on a stone cross,
the old master writes
his own epitaph . . .
only to be forgotten
like the wind and rain

Vasile Moldovan, Bucharest, Romania

coloring
inside the line
of a perfectly round moon
she remembers
her dead mother

Elisa Theriana, Bandung, Indonesia

how deep
is my sorrow
not seeing my mother
before she passed away?
I gaze at a sea painting

Nu Quang, Seattle, WA

dying oak tree . . .
still there are stories
to be told
as her acorns
remain

Roy Kindelberger, Edmonds, WA

a hawk
with outstretched wings
dead in our backyard
the chatter of gatherings
from years ago

Mary Davila, Buffalo, NY

it's been twenty years
since Father left
the boat had disappeared
yet I still feel some ripples
from the wake

Elinor Pihl Huggett, Lakeville, IN

another cold winter
in the old folks' home
she still folds
the daily paper
his way

Jodie Hawthorne, Kaohsiung City, Taiwan

two decades . . .
still so hard
to say goodbye
I rearrange
mother's cupboard

Madhuri Pillai, Melbourne, Australia

dew drops
on crimson nasturtium
how my aborted baby
calls me
from unknown lands

Arvinder Kaur, Chandigarh, India

jars of pulque
the color of milk . . .
grandfather's spirit
ferments on a shelf
in the old shed

Victor Ortiz, Bellingham, WA

what will become of us?
pieces of driftwood
overlooked on the shore
or perhaps a favourite shell
still whispering in your ear

Joanna Ashwell, Barnard Castle, UK

in a ghost town
an abandoned church
hidden by kudzu
spots of daylight
flicker inside

John Zheng, Itta Bena, MS

October brings
its memories of loss—
how beautiful
the bloodgrass
in this cold wind

Ce Rosenow, Eugene, OR

this first spring
after my sister's death
how green
the new grass
over her grave

Edward J. Rielly, Westbrook, ME

foggy morning
I gather winter greens
for his tombstone
all the questions
I never asked

Marilyn Ashbaugh, Edwardsburg, MI

the years it has taken
for this grief to resolve . . .
each day
as the leaves fall
I see the sky more clearly

Rebecca Drouilhet, Picayune, MS

Tanka Sequences

Sanctuary

Debbie Strange, Winnipeg, MB, Canada

how soft,
my grandfather's cheek
he shows me
the little swans inside
every columbine

I sift seeds
between my fingers
scattering them
like prayers offered
to the sun and rain

moon-pennies
set the dark alight
I leave a trail
of petals for you
to spend come morning

welcome
to my garden oasis
every blossom
was once a sorrow buried
deep inside the earth

On His Birthday

Gerry Jacobson, Canberra, Australia

living on the edge
of the universe
'now'
shimmers into existence
one moment at a time

in the park
this summer evening
the shadow
of past winters
and that which might come

time seems
to flow right past me
but am I
the same 'me'
at all these times

clinging on
but everything changes
death
is certain . . .
or could it be recycling?

culling books
giving away clothes
preparing
to go naked
into the next life

Tanka String Quartet

Neal Whitman, Pacific Grove, CA

giving the downbeat—
so, you think you're in charge
first violin
after Thanksgiving dinner
I take out the garbage

understanding
the emotional context
second violin
the night of my senior prom
I play second fiddle

sadly
looked down upon by others
viola
often the brunt of a joke
I hold my head up high

only one
capable of lower notes
cello
easy going and pleasant
I get along with the in-laws

A Provençal Cherry Orchard

Giselle Maya, St. Martin de Castillon, France

a breeze
in our flowing hair
for a brief spell
we touch the kami
of snow-white blossom

cherry orchard
now cut down–
not long ago
we danced among petals
our laughter taken by the wind

may poets survive
to write of forests, deer and fowls
a flourishing planet
where Greta's children
leap into spring

Gallipoli Visit

Marilyn Humbert, Sydney, Australia

Kilitbahir fortress*
emerges from dawn mist
. . . on the ferry
crossing the Dardanelles
we sip thick black coffee

our bus
follows rugged coastline
shadowing
steady marching columns
of WW1 soldiers

forested slopes
of Gaba Tepe soar **
from the beach
—the Turkish
hold the high ground

we listen
for sounds of battle
the voices of soldiers
—a cold wind
haunts these hills

trenches
half-filled now
echo with dreams
boys lost from both sides
names engraved on memorials

*ancient castle opposite the town of Canakkale on the Dardanelles
Strait, Turkey
**landing site, known by Allies as ANZAC Cove

Awash In Dreams

Carol Raisfeld, Atlantic Beach, NY

your voice
nestles in my ear
like a secret . . .
I recall it at will
inside a dream

playing back
your words,
warm yet fleeting
the sun in and out
along the shore

afloat
on moonlit waves
we drift
back and forth
caught in the middle

we become one
desire tethered to desire
you tug back
sinking the hook deeper
the sand rearranged

Long Distance Love

Amelia Fielden, Belconnen, ACT, Australia

sixteen nights
of the surf sighing
and my grandson
sleeping in the next bed . . .
sixteen summer nights

no rain for weeks . . .
now Eastern rosellas
fluttering
in puddles on the path,
bright brollies at the bus stop

growling
round my house, the west wind
grows fiercer—
another winter
of long distance love

apple blossom
blown off, scattering
who knows where—
the magnolia tree
clasps its crimson flowers

guardian
of my grandchildren,
Mt. Rainier
soars snow-topped below
my flight from far away

Sakura Sash

Mari Konno, Fukui, Japan

petals
from cherry blossoms
falling
onto an azure lake
news of her illness

sitting
by the evening harbor
I held my friend's hand
the color of sunset
slipping away

photograph
of your usual smile
on the altar
I wonder which is real
her smile or my tears

mountain
capped with snow
and wild geese
gliding over the lake
my first winter without you

the sakura sash
you used to wear
at tea ceremonies
I wrap it around
my memories of you

Coming on Two Years

Adelaide B. Shaw, Somers, NY

your photo
pauses my movement
each time I look;
there are no skipped days
in missing you

I should have known
that expectations were false
that time would run
not a marathon
but a sprint

regrets I have
and pricks of guilt
for chances lost;
perhaps forgiveness comes
in the afterlife

Miriam

Kathryn J. Stevens, Cary, NC

we hid behind
the ivy-covered fence,
with the cat as witness
we linked pinkies and swore
best friends forever

your illness
takes a bit more
every day
beyond the window
rain pale as twilight

I hold your hand
as the moon rises
and talk about small things
bare trees, melting snow
somewhere a clock ticks

streaming rain
blackens the ridge
stripping this day of color
another loved one
is leaving me behind

I see you still
walking head bent
down the trail
red jacket snapping
in an errant wind

Fire

Sara Ellison, Sebastopol, CA

on a bright mid-afternoon
an orange flutter
a monarch passing
into the shade
behind the house

a flash of memory
untamed
bright flames
burn through the night
into a dawn with no sun

I feel lost in
this changed place
where wild oat grass
and oil spiced eucalyptus
inspire fear not solace

there is a quiet place
in the bones
where heaviness lives
the earth bears
our weight of loss

Responsive Tanka

Resolutions

Kath Abela Wilson, Pasadena, CA
Jackie Chou, Pico Rivera, CA

his last days
I left the door to our home
wide open
nothing worse
could come in

between her last words
rays of skylight
shining through
the many doors
to her legacy

after he died
I thought I'd lock the door
stay alone
as yet unknown
my heart's instinct

through sinuous paths
of my current life
I find my way
into the arms
of forbidden love

past and future
merge on the tree of life
like jackfruit
in the garden of eden
being picked

walking alone
where she once held my hand
the road ahead
opened up
to brand new destinies

cherry moon

Paresh Tiwara, India and *Pamela A. Babusci, USA*

just beyond
the whiteness of fog
a swallowtail . . .
the colours of dawn
cling to my fingertips

your brevity of love
is fleeting like a moth
to a flame . . .
will you ever cleave to
the paleness of flesh?

floating like
an unmoored cloud
i have lost
and found myself
on your unpainted lips

i am at the mercy
of your fiery
hunger
cherry moon rising
over an iron mountain

knowing that
at least for today
we are in love
i wake up to the soft
warmth of your curls

Tanka Prose

Introduction

Through These Eyes

> taking readers
> on a journey--
> physical or emotional
> --not just because it happened
> but because it truly matters *

If tanka prose is a journey, and I think it is, then I'm not surprised that, as I meditate on the poems for this issue, I'm drawn to their landscapes. Exterior landscapes with telling detail, down to the barnacles on sea-swept rocks. That drafty barn glimpsed from the road; deer among river birch; the caterpiller on milkweed; a robin chirruping above the stream. Interior views can also shape a journey: bus passengers anonymous behind their papers; poker machines, row on row, in a gaming parlor; the plant jungle in a child's room.

And there's the emotional journey, the soulscape. As poet Kat Lehman puts it, "I love the balance of scene-setting and lyrical openness provided by tanka prose." This emotional openness draws a reader in and makes the story matter. Contributors to this section have generously shared their feelings, their vulnerability.

In this tanka community, we reach out to each other across the pages. With that in mind, I invited contributors to share something about their creative process. I felt privileged to know them better through the backstories of their work. I hope you'll feel the same.

Kat Lehman's poem is the first of several reflecting on our relationship with the physical world around us. Until recently, she dwelt in a house with a "river at the bottom of the hill" that became, she writes, "part of my healing journey through difficult times: its beauty, its white noise, and the simple reminders it brought about life's cycles."

Love of the natural world often pairs with appreciation for rural landscapes. As **Adelaide B. Shaw** notes, barns "are the heart and soul of a farm, housing and [protecting] animals and equipment." Having lived in the country with barns of all kinds around her, she often photographed them to create haiga.

Practitioners of Zen meditation, **Sally Biggar** and her husband spent almost three decades in Port Townsend on Washington's Olympic Peninsula. They offered public meditations at their home twice-monthly to reach out to people who observe a range of meditation traditions. She describes a ceremony in her Moon Garden that speaks of respect for the earth. It was led by a group member who wanted to bless everyone with rituals "he'd been learning from Lakota elders . . . . We had this 'braid' of traditions at work . . . as we honored our search for meaning in this difficult life with an American Indian blessing," under the watchful eye of a garden statue, Quan Yin, the Buddhist goddess of compassion.

David Rice speaks plainly about the planet in "Homework." "I've been consumed with trying to figure out how to respond to the climate crisis from a psychological (spiritual, if you will) perspective, as well as from a practical/behavioral point of view," he writes. "How does the climate crisis affect our relationships to those who are coming after us, as well as those who came before?"

Deer season was fast upon him when **P.O. Fieweger** began writing. In Wisconsin, he says, "the deer hunt is a huge deal. People take vacation days to participate, drive long distances, lay out large sums of cash, and stores designate 'Orange Friday' specifically for hunters." A vegetarian who practices Zen, Fieweger believes "the way society abuses food animals is immoral. And to use animals for sport . . ."

We enter the writing world with a former sports reporter's take on football and glory dreams. **Bob Loomis** notes he pared down his longer original, changing perspective to give it new relevancy.

Being in a writing group figures in "Downhill" by **Keitha Keyes**. "I've tried to give some background to . . . a very disturbing experience," she says. "And I still wrestle with my conscience-- should I have . . . stopped to reconnect? Could I have made a difference?"

An Alaskan, **Teri White Carns** had the "good fortune to take an online haibun class with Allegra Wong. Joan and Gabrielle from Melbourne, who write novels, book reviews, and a blog [as] 'Gert Loveday,'" were also in the class. They became friends and planned to take Allegra's tanka prose class, but it didn't work out. Then in 2018, Carns and her family "went to Melbourne to meet 'the Gerts,' who took us to a friend's home in the hills outside Nar Nar Goon in the Shire of Cardinia. Another day we drove out the Great Ocean Road to bluffs above the sea . . . This is my thanks to Allegra, and to Gert Loveday."

Would we be writers if we didn't love to read? "There's nothing like the feel of the page as I browse," **Carol Raisfeld** writes. "A bookstore . . . is a place of quiet contemplation, self-discovery, and treasure seeking. It allows us to enter a completely different world."

Contemplation turns further inward with **Joy McCall**'s haunting tanka prose. "I do a lot of musing these days about spirit and body and how they connect," she says. "Life as a bedbound paralyzed woman is very different from 'normality.' They say that walking upright defines us as human beings. It's the thing I lost seventeen years ago and I still grieve the loss. My spirit is fine. My body is not. That's all I know."

"Out of Control" explores a tenuous, isolating world. **Grix** comments: "As a survivor of domestic abuse and one who lives with debilitating chronic pain, I wished to juxtapose the two [to help] readers understand the retraumatization that occurs for many who live with chronic medical conditions. Lack of dominion over our own bodies while having to rely on family and medical personnel for . . . basic functions can be very traumatizing. For people who've been abused, getting . . . medical care can trigger flashbacks of the original trauma."

Relationships also figure in "Sink or Swim." **Liz Lanagan**'s weekly writing group typically has a facilitator, and the "prompt of rings" inspired this piece. The engagement ring's circular image morphs into the inflatable inner tube in the tanka that, in turn, ties into the title.

Xenia Tran's "The Pier at Findochty" came out of a day trip to this quaint fishing village on the Moray coast. After a walk around the quay with her husband and two dogs, Tran "paused beside the sculpture of the seated Fisherman overlooking the harbour. [It] has a comforting presence, and after . . . a while it felt as if he was a real person. I followed his gaze . . . . This is when the poem came to me."

Emigration and travel shape several poems. His mother's nightmare on the eve of his emigration to Canada inspired **Chen-ou Liu**: She dreamed she "stood holding me in her arms helplessly, unable to see anything ahead of her, for she was enveloped by darkness . . . [A] pain rose from her feet and gradually up to her shoulders and arms. [At] the point of almost despair, suddenly, a spot of bright space appeared by her side. She used her last ounce of strength to put me down while I remained sound asleep. As soon as I was laid on the ground, the earth unexpectedly began to tilt . . . . [C]areening down, I suddenly grew up, and within a few minutes was no larger than a speck of dust." (From his haibun, "Our Dreams," published in *Simply Haiku*, Spring 2011.)

Of "Encounter, 1969" **Margaret Chula** relates: "I was young and eager for adventure, so I signed up" for a British-American secretarial exchange through Brook Street Bureau. "The bureau found jobs for us as temps and also [unsubsidized] housing. One of my memorable experiences was attending a polo match and afternoon tea with Queen Elizabeth and Prince Philip." A Buckingham Palace maid obtained and donated an invitation to the bureau. "Out of all the secretaries, my name was picked out of the hat! So . . . I was lucky in a number of ways."

Her Hertfordshire city north of London is the setting for **Iliyana Stoyanova**'s tanka prose. "It was born while walking in town . . . As a Christian, the holiday season has a very special meaning to me but . . . over the years . . . things have been changing around us. And not for the best. During my walk it felt like I was taking part in a Beckett-like theatrical performance, so absurd and surreal. Where was the true spirit of Christmas, the true giving?"

Marcyn Clements's "Wind in the Pass" lifts the spirits, with its migrating Demoiselle cranes that rise above the Tien Shan Mountains in Kazakhstan. Clements traveled there to see the wild tulips, including one variety with "two flowers on each of two stems. [This is] where tulips originated . . . On the mountains and high passes, and in wild plains, they [still] grow untended, some highly endemic and endangered."

> blue heron
> lend me your wings
> the hill rises
> steep
> and long

> *—Susan Weaver*

*My found tanka is taken (with permission) from Autumn Noelle Hall's essay, "Tanka Prose: A Hail and How-To," *Ribbons*, Spring/Summer 2017.

River Therapy
Kat Lehmann, Guilford, CT

You seemed indifferent to me, like an endless flock of geese flying south, until you carried my worries downstream and away. I wasn't even seeking you, but there you were, beyond the archway, down the hill past the river birch, behind the growth of nameless green. The seasonal home to geese, deer. And, now, me.

opening my mouth
to the autumn rain
I take in
the end of the old cycle
the beginning of the next

Prime Real Estate
Adelaide B. Shaw, Somers, NY

I love barns. Clean, glossy, show-case barns. Mud-spattered, peeling paint, loose board barns. Broken window, holes in the roof barns. Red, blue, gray, green with metal roofs, shingle roofs, collapsed roofs. Modern barns and abandoned ones, home to the wind, birds, vines, cobwebs, dirt and dust . . .

for sale
open concept home—
empty barn
drafty doors and leaky roof
bedroom loft with hay mattress

A Drop of Dew

Sally Biggar, Topsham, ME

In our garden, the statue of Quan Yin beckons. We form a circle around her. Casey lights a sweetgrass braid, begins to chant in Lakota. I don't understand the words, but there is power in his prayer, and I feel it. Using an eagle's wing, he fans sweet smoke over each one of us.

Casey walks the Red Road now, but he was not born into it. Quan Yin's quiet presence is a perfect complement to his Lakota blessing ceremony for the new year. She is the Chinese Goddess of Compassion. It is said her heart melts at our sorrow. Even before you utter your plea, Quan Yin has heard you, and responded. She holds my gaze throughout our ceremony.

> such a tranquil face
> yet . . . one luminous
> drop of dew
> quivers on her eyelid
> ready to fall

Casey lights his *chanupa*. Smoking is the Lakota way to communicate with the spirit realm. As we pass his pipe, Casey continues to chant. Smoke curls through cypress branches and gradually fades into the ashen sky.

Homework

David Rice, Berkeley, CA

Read the spiritual teachers. We're not separate from nature. If the forests, oceans, and deserts are besieged, we're besieged. Nurture nature, nurture ourselves. Do something to help.

> Sierra forest
> beetle-browned
> and silent
> we could plant more pines . . .
> would they die, too?

If our war with the earth ends a hundred years from now, what will the peace treaty look like? Native Americans lived with nature. Then the Euro-Americans arrived.

> the last Native American Yahi
> family massacred
> walked into Oroville one day—
> never told anyone
> his name

Care for nature the way we would if it were our child. Proceed with equanimity and compassion despite ongoing cataclysms. Take the long view. Focus on what you can do. Make that enough.

> granddaughter
> growing a plant jungle
> in her room
> *I'm improving air quality*
> twelve-year-old activist

The Hunt

P.O. Fieweger, West Bend, WI

brown fields
and thickets
stark woods
under leaden skies
the land is silent

Late November in Wisconsin is a time of austere beauty. Nature is at peace. It is also the setting for the annual nine-day whitetail deer hunt. In blaze orange, men and women, but overwhelmingly men, invade woods and fields. They may spread out and drive the deer, but most often they occupy pre-selected tree stands and blinds to pit their skills with high-powered rifles against an animal whose only natural defenses are its wariness and speed.

a thunderous shot
slams into the silence
heads go up
searching the air for
vaguely recalled dangers

For some the hunt is tradition passed down from fathers. For others it is an opportunity to stock larders with venison steaks and sausage. And for yet others it is a social affair, the opportunity to hang out and drink with buddies for nine days. Killing is a bonus. But for all, a successful hunt bestows bragging rights.

stale smoke
loud music
and laughter
it was magnificent
one shot through the heart

Over the years I've heard more blow-by-blow tales than I care to consider. How the wily hunter exhibited skill and the patience of a saint waiting for the perfect buck with the perfect rack, or any deer for that matter, to come down the trail. Then there is the all important shot that drops the animal where it stands. Only, more times than not, it stumbles, wounded, and takes off running. The hunter must then track it. If the deer has run more than a few hundred feet without collapsing, or there is insufficient snow for tracking, or darkness falls, there's little chance of success.

> gunshots roll
> across harvested fields
> deer scatter
> how many will die
> slow painful deaths this night

Gridiron Dreams

Bob Loomis, Concord, CA

Reading of the latest findings correlating repeated blows to the head in football with early memory loss, I recall how badly I wanted to be a football hero as a young man. This desire lasted about four years, including two years of going out for the team at Los Angeles City College.

As it happened, I lacked the physical gifts and skills to become the hero I wanted to be, so I became a sports reporter instead. Apparently, I may have been more fortunate than I realized. I am now eighty and still have most of my memory marbles. As far as I know.

> old high school jersey
> same number as the football star
> I tried to emulate
> if anyone hit me that hard now
> I'd be dead meat

Downhill

Keitha Keyes, Sydney, NSW, Australia

Once a week I walk through the gaming section of a club to get to a meeting in another room. In the gaming room are rows and rows of poker machines. Even at 9 o'clock in the morning, most of the machines have been claimed.

Last week I saw someone there that I recognized. And here he is again today. A man I knew from a writing group who had a real talent for short stories, many of which were published. A generous mentor for other writers.

I wonder why he is playing the poker machines so early in the day. Does he come here every day? Is he in some sort of financial trouble? Has his marriage broken down? Does he write anymore?

> in the half light
> a shadow of a man
> hunched over
> staring at a screen
> . . . is this his life now?

Southern Cross Station, Melbourne

Teri White Carns, Anchorage, AK

> barnacles clinging
> to rocks edging the south sea
> tides washing in, out—
> we sit at picnic tables
> feeding sweet crumbs to black ants

We become acquainted in a long-distance writing class, separated by the waters between the Gulf of Alaska and the Tasmanian Sea. Today, I meet them at the Melbourne station named after the stars that light their skies. On the train to Geelong, we talk about kangaroos along the roads, fall clothes for Easter, sled dogs, our children.

We walk the path on the bluff in the Great Otways National Park. Scrub and small flowers line the way above red cliffs that gave up their ochre for Wadawurrung ceremonies, and after that to color English railroad cars. Tiny surfers rest on the swells at Bell's Beach hundreds of feet below.

At the lighthouse café, we quiet our stomachs with sandwiches in the shade of a tree. We swelter in the late summer heat, brush away flies. I am entranced, intimidated, wanting to preserve the veil of romance and strangeness, and still be easy friends, with the comfort of people known for a lifetime.

> fresh plum cake
> stone Ganesh in a reed-filled pond
> harvest days
> these new friends too soon let go
> petals giving way to fruit

The Days Before

Carol Raisfeld, Atlantic Beach, NY

Bookstores will always remain a place of wonder to me. Like libraries, they hold the world's longest, most exhilarating conversation. The people who work in them will put in your hand something you just have to read, by someone you've never heard of, someone entering the conversation, who wants to talk about something important.

At midnight, my urge to browse literary choices and read reviews got the better of me, resulting in a solitary point and click. In that moment I surrendered to the online retailer's chilly embrace.

> in a journey
> of deep dreams
> too soon
> I wake to the blankness
> of morning

Levels

Joy McCall, Norwich, England

I sit on the low levels of old Maslow's hierarchy, watching the
comings and goings of things above my head.

> now and then a hand
> reaches down and pulls me up
> to sit awhile
> where the air is clean and rare
> and full of quietness

> then the lead weights
> swing again and I slip
> slowly back down
> into the milling crowd
> my head full of confusion

> how the days
> turn into ash down here
> in the careless firepits
> the smoke rises up and up
> through the hopeful spaces

I look up at the bright light, shining through that small gap at the
top, filtering through the dark shadows down to this dusty ground.
One day I'll look down on it all and watch . . .

> the faint thin smoke
> of the burned days and nights
> rising
> like pleadings and prayers
> to the wide empty sky

Out of Control
Grix, Wilmington, DE

"Where are you going? Who are you going with? You just went out on Monday! You can't leave me; you're nobody without me!"

I pinch the skin on the back of my hand as hard as I can—an attempt to drown out your voice. I've done everything you've asked of me; I've catered to your every whim. I arrange my hours, days, weeks, and months around you to avoid making you angry. I let you know well in advance and make all of the necessary arrangements to put you at ease. Still, every time I want to do something without you, you make it clear who's calling the shots.

immobilized
by fiery pain—
stuck in bed again,
appeasing
my demon

Sink or Swim
Liz Lanigan, Canberra, Australia

I say all the right things. "Congratulations. Show me your ring. Oh, it's beautiful. That diamond. Wow. And what a stylish setting." Then he walks in. I come so close to blurting it out. How her husband-to-be had come on to me just last week. But she's snuggling into his shoulder, looking so happy.

round her waist
a gaudy coloured
blow-up ring . . .
how to keep afloat
until she learns to swim

The Pier at Findochty
Xenia Tran, Nairn, Scotland

Most of the sailing boats are on the quayside, masts folded. Fresh paintwork glitters in the morning sun. There is still the odd ice patch, in the shadows of the harbour. A small dog slips as he scampers up the brae.

watching over us
a seated fisherman
full of stories
my eyes begin to wander
past the lighthouse, out to sea

The Point of No Return
Chen-ou Liu, Ajax, ON, Canada

On the day of my emigration to Canada, a land of maple leaves and snowflakes that will eventually bury my past.

a parting
of summer clouds
mother
lets go of my hand
. . . and of my heart

Encounter, 1969

Margaret Chula, Portland, OR

I'm sitting in the back seat of the cheerful red London bus. The faces of my fellow passengers are hidden in the folds of the *London Times*. I'm twenty-one and terrified. The bus growls and squeaks. I begin to cry, sniffles at first, then sobs muffled into shredded tissues.

Are you okay? the blond woman next to me asks. Her features are delicate, her eyes blue, like mine, her accent American.

My travel agency went out of business, I tell her. *The bursar absconded with the funds. I have no ticket back to Boston and not enough money to buy another.* We both disembark at Kensington Church Street, where I share a flat with four English girls.

She holds my hand as we walk along streets with brightly-lit shop windows. *I want to stay longer in London,* she says. *You can have my ticket and stay at my flat in Cambridge. Pay me back when you get a job.*

I buy her a scone, and we share a pot of English breakfast tea. Her name is Gina. We were born on the same day, the same month, and in the same year.

> when I was seven
> I found a whole patch
> of four-leaf clovers—
> that day I knew
> I'd always be blessed

Heart Break
Gerry Jacobson, Canberra, Australia

I don't know why he turns against me. I think we are best friends. Well, we probably are for a year or two. At the age of nine or eleven. We are both among the few Jewish boys in primary school. His parents are refugees from Germany, as my mum is. So she is friendly with them. They live around the corner from us.

My memory fades. I'm struggling to recall a few details. We go to different high schools. His parents anglicise their name. Do his parents split up?

Just one thing. I remember knocking on his door one day and his mum is apologetic, trying to explain that he has other friends now. That he goes to a Jewish youth club. I turn away. I turn inwards.

skimming
this morning's newspaper
suddenly
jolted awake
by the death notices

In the Eyes of Others
Alexander Jankiewicz, Dixon, IL

. . . I feel gratitude in my heart each time I can meet someone and look at his or her smile. —Elie Wiesel

"It's just unnatural and shouldn't be allowed,"grumbles an old man at the table next to ours at the train station's outdoor cafe. "In the old days, they'd be . . . sent away."

"Oh, be quiet and finish your streusel," the old woman he's with says curtly.

The two young women he's referring to have been happily talking at a nearby table while holding hands, when one kisses the other. They couldn't be a more mismatched pair, with one being full-out goth and the other dressed in a gray, conservative pant suit.

"It's just not proper," he insists under his breath before taking a loud slurp from his coffee. "This is something dirty."

A police officer walks up to the women's table.

"Look, he'll put a stop to this," the old man says.

"There you are! I know you two sisters haven't seen each other in such a long time," the officer remarks in a joyful tone, "but your mother is waiting for you at home. Come now! She's been preparing your favorite meal all afternoon!"

"Yes, Papa," the two say in unison and immediately stand up.

After a moment of silence, the old woman looks at her companion, shaking her head. "You should be ashamed of yourself."

"But I didn't know," he replies.

"And what difference does that make?" she demands.

When she stands and reaches out to collect her purse, I notice the tattoo on her forearm.

> before dawn
> a cherry blossom falls
> in darkness
> birdsong gathers
> waiting for the sun to rise

Babble and Whispers

Iliyana Stoyanova, St Albans, UK

I stop briefly in a little garden on the way to the High Street. The gentle twilight steals a few moments from my precious last-minute shopping time. Torn between ephemeral drawings of clouds over the horizon and my duties, I carry on.

In front of a local theatre, I almost stumble over a rack of chairs with a note stuck on them: "Take me home for Xmas." The slight slope and my fast pace make me breathe deeper, and I feel high from the winter air. For a moment I forget I'm in the old town and transpose myself to the mountains; I see snow-covered pines and frozen lakes.

The familiar din of the High Street brings me back to reality. I slalom between eager chuggers* and other shoppers, some with smiling faces, others already bored by the Christmas chores of gift buying and spreading good will. In front of a glitzy boutique, a homeless person sits invisible to the crowds around him, a pile of discounted biscuits and croissants his festive meal tonight. A young couple argue whether to get some cards, the "cheap stuff," in order to have money left for booze.

It's only 4 p.m. and yet already feels like night-time. Decorations flicker up in the trees, public post boxes topped with hand knitted ornaments attract the flashes of mobile phones, and people seem to be getting into the spirit of the holidays.

Or do they? Next to one of the post boxes, a young man in a loud Christmas sweater shouts something that sounds like cursing. Then I see his badge: I have Asperger's. He is handing out free puzzle games and in-between profanities he yells, "Make puzzles NOT war."

winter wind
your thousand kisses turn into
snowflakes
a true sign
God watches over us

* chugger (charity mugger) — a person employed by a charity organisation to solicit donations

Raw Edge

Ann Corbett Burke, Orefield, PA

This is the day I have been longing for, the margin between winter and spring, sunshiny and cold but not excruciatingly so.

I should be out in the bright garden planting onions but am still in my pajamas at 3 p.m. because my good friend's husband is dying and I think about me, me, me on the day my own husband died three years ago. Today I can do nothing to help—my friend or myself—so I cook and drink and cry. Create, obliterate, release . . . start again.

> hollow reeds
> stand at the stream
> edged in frost—
> on a nearby tree
> a robin sings

Metamorphosis

Marilyn Fleming, Pewaukee, WI

Today is one of those introspective days in early autumn. A tinge of vermilion is in the leaves, and the sun feels warm. There is a pungent earthy scent in the air. I notice a monarch as it alights on a stem of lavender, opening and closing its wings, and it makes me happy.

It was years ago when I was awakened early on a Sunday morning with a phone call from my mother. *My sister was killed in a car crash.* We were a year apart, almost like twins. Odd how one phone call can change a life. Nothing was ever the same.

I was in shock and zombie-like for a long time. One day during my zombie-time, the neighbor brought me a caterpillar that he had found on a nearby twig with a leaf still attached. I put it in a jar with air holes in the lid and crossed my fingers. I checked on it daily as it devoured the leaf and slowly formed a pupa. The sun came up fourteen times and the sun went down thirteen times before I began to notice a change.

> my breath stops—
> a monarch
> emerges
> from the chrysalis
> wet wings folded

At daybreak she opened her wings. I carefully removed her from the jar, still attached to the twig, and carried her outside. Imagine my joy when she settled on my hand and then, ever so slowly, began circling me. She lingered a few hours, then gracefully fluttered off.

> your eyelashes
> on my eyelashes
> awakened
> with butterfly kisses
> her face fades away

Wind in the Pass

Marcyn Clements, Claremont, CA

The Demoiselles are only passing through. Hundreds of them out in the fallow fields. They fly down in groups of twenty and thirty. Land and bow, ruffle their flight feathers. Throw back their graceful necks. Posture and prance. Soon they will lift their lines of migrating wings. Rise above the Tien Shan Mountains. Turn and head north, along the lakes and plains and sand dunes, high over tulip meadows beyond the Urals. To breed in Russia, somewhere in the far north of this planet. The smallest crane in the world.

> tiny pale tulips
> bend their two-necked heads
> in the wind
> of Kuyuk Pass
> in Kazakhstan

Poet and Tanka

My Tanka Journey
Michael H. Lester

Growing up with no understanding of poetry and having acquired a lifelong distaste for it in school, imagine my shock when I discover more than half a century later, not only do I like poetry, I am in fact a poet myself!

I start slowly with mostly rhyming poems. Perusing a website called RhymeZone, I notice there is a contest and decide to enter a poem. I don't win or even get an honorable mention, but I do become involved in a public forum where I post poems, get and give feedback, and make some poet friends.

One of these friends introduces the forum to haiku, and another introduces the forum to tanka. After a bit of research, I write my first tanka, a titled, 5-7-5-7-7 poem, and post it to the group.

Fried Dumplings

The hungry wolves howled
silhouetted by dour moon
scaring the children
who ran, laughing hyenas
to my hut for fried dumplings

After about one year as an active member of the Rhymezone forum, I decide it is time to look for journals where I can submit my poems for publication. I soon discover the tanka journals. One of my first submissions is a tanka prose to *Ribbons*. Janet Lynn Davis rejects my submission but gives me valuable feedback and a referral to a forum called Inkstone. I immediately join, a membership I value and maintain to this day. In Inkstone, I rub shoulders with and learn from some of the top tankaists in Asian short-form poetry. I credit Janet with my immersion into the world of tanka and consider her my first tanka mentor.

Autumn Noelle Hall rejects another of my tanka prose submissions and, like Janet, gives me valuable feedback. Autumn and I become friends and collaborators for a time, publishing some of our work in *Atlas Poetica* and another journal. I consider Autumn to be my second tanka mentor.

In 2017, I enter the Tanka Society of America's Sanford Goldstein International Tanka Contest and win an honorable mention for this poem:

> etched
> on a totem pole
> in Apache
> screeching owl
> loves quiet mouse

The first feather in my tanka cap and I am thrilled!

Soon after TSA announces the winners, I receive a Facebook message from another honorable mention poet, Joy McCall, congratulating me on my poem. I notice Joy's name a lot on Facebook, in tanka journals, as a prolific author of tanka books, and as a frequent collaborator with various other tanka poets. She is evidently a beloved tanka poet in this community. I ask Joy if she would collaborate with me and she agrees.

Our first collaboration is a long supernatural tanka sequence, which we write over a few days by email and submit for publication. Although this collaboration does not find a publisher, we have fun and now correspond daily, sharing our lives, our fears, our trials, and our poems. Joy is a constant and consistent confidence booster for me. She gently guides me back to tanka when I stray to other poetic forms, finally convincing me that tanka is where I belong. Joy is my third mentor and the most influential person in my poetic life.

After a time, Joy introduces me to Sanford Goldstein and encourages me to correspond with him. Sanford and I exchange tanka for a few weeks, some of which M. Kei publishes in his tanka journal, *Atlas Poetica*. I continue to enter the Goldstein contest, winning honorable mention in 2018, and second place and honorable mention in 2019.

This brings me to M. Kei, a tanka scholar, a fine tanka poet, and the editor of *Atlas Poetica*, a journal of international tanka. Kei's philosophy as an editor, unlike other tanka journals, is to publish a lot of work from contributing poets so that readers of the journal can get a better sense of what the poet has to say and how they say it. Kei generously affords me the opportunity to edit two special features for the journal, 25 Rhyming Kyoka, and 25 Death Poems. I consider Kei my patron saint and the second most important influence in my poetic life.

Kei believes that a tanka is simply "a short lyric poem originally from Japan composed of five poetic phrases conventionally written on five lines in English." I have adopted this definition as my own guide to writing tanka. I have experimented with many forms and styles of tanka, but I cannot say that the tanka I write are influenced by any particular tanka poet or tanka style. I am a tanka rebel with a style peculiar to myself, and that is just the way I like it.

I constantly question what I am doing in this tanka world, what I should be doing, and what I want to be doing, sometimes happily and sometimes not so much.

> it helps
> every once in a while
> to pick up
> a brittle twig
> and snap it in two

The following is a selection of some of my other favorite tanka written in the few years I've been on this tanka journey.

broken oaks
waiting patiently to die
for someone
to count their rings
and tell their stories

Second Place, 2019 Sanford Goldstein International Tanka Contest

to comfort me
when the crickets go quiet
the murmuring
of a thousand streams
trickling down the mountain

Honorable Mention, Fujisan Taisho Tanka Festival 2019

I soothe my brittle bones
where the river cleaves in two
and bathe
in the quiet serenity
of a pale harvest moon

International Tanka Society Journal, No. 3, 2018

her face
pale as alabaster
dissipates
my lips still savoring
the merciful kiss of death

Tanka Society of America, Fall edition
of The Tanka Café, *Ribbons* 2018

the wind whistles
like an eerie ghost train
through a tunnel
filled with wailing apparitions
bemoaning their final journey

International Tanka Society Journal, No. 5, 2019

an old junk
rattles over choppy seas
brown, wrinkled hands
tie knots in frayed ropes
and the moon bleeds yellow

International Tanka Society Journal, No. 4, 2019

water buffalo
graze along the riverbank
tail-flicking flies
she guides my clumsy hand
with a faraway look

Atlas Poetica, No. 35, 2018

dressed in violet
redolent of the scent
of watercress
she leaves dainty footprints
in the frothy white sand

The Bamboo Hut, Summer 2019

he has become
quite cantankerous
in his old age
but the grandchildren
would never know it

All the Way Home: Aging in Haiku, A Robert Epstein Anthology,
Middle Island Press, 2019

Book Reviews

In my new capacity as book review editor, I would like to extend warm and delighted greetings to readers of *Ribbons* and all members of the TSA. I am honored to have been granted this opportunity (many thanks to David Rice for inviting me to be the next book review editor) and look forward to doing my best to illuminate and analyze contemporary works of tanka, in addition to books of general interest to tanka poets, through detailed and high-quality reviews. My style as a reviewer—as an outgrowth of my approach as a reader and in writing my own poems—emphasizes quality over quantity, depth over breadth. The crux of my duties entails striking a comfortable balance between these approaches; I hope to prove capable of doing so, and humbly request your patience, dear readers and fellow enthusiasts of all things tanka-related, while I find my footing and settle into that balance, in the meantime.

—*Tamara K. Walker*

Edward J. Rielly's Bed of Geraniums
Tamara K. Walker

Edward J. Rielly. *A Bed of Geraniums*. Farmington, Maine: Encircle Publications, 2019. ISBN: 978-1-64599-031-4. Paperback, 45 pages, $14.95 at http://encirclepub.com/.

A Bed of Geraniums, the latest book of poetry by award-winning poet and English professor emeritus Edward J. Rielly, is an autobiographical and retrospective collection of tanka that reflect on the poet's past stages of life and present concerns from the vantage point of advanced age, joining the ranks of a sort of sub-genre of personal tanka collections that includes David Rice's warmly pensive *The Grandfather Poems* and Randy Brooks' buoyant and unvarnished *Walking the Fence*. Rielly's tanka, organized in four sections, lyrically and movingly encapsulate perceptive and contemplative meditations on subjects including fleeting sensory glimpses rendered meaningful by understated wisdom, childhood reminiscence, familial relationships and much in between.

Of initial note is the book's splendid physical design. While subpar or bland cover art and construction rarely detract much from tanka collections, outstanding design can certainly enhance the reading experience, and befitting its floral title, this book is beautiful, with shimmering bronze-gold flyleaves, a visually appealing cover and well-chosen fonts. Its attractive appearance is a perfect prelude to the tanka of a poet whose acute command of visual imagery is exquisite, and whose quiet but affecting poetic voice and presence in a range of crystalline moments is vividly evocative.

One of the most noteworthy facets of this collection is Rielly's use of color, both as a general concept and when referencing individual hues. The first section, "for a few more days," begins with a tanka that depicts a sunset in surprisingly original images:

> slowly the sun sinks
> into the ocean . . .
> water boiling
> in a cauldron
> of rainbow colors

This poem symbolically sets the tone for the book to follow, in which the setting sun of the poet's golden years gives rise to an iridescent spectrum of tanka. Elsewhere, color itself is a backdrop for completely implicit and resigned lament of natural evanescence that almost calls to mind classical waka in its sensibility:

> the flowers
> I nurtured into
> a rainbow of colors
> now brown and brittle
> turning, also, to dust

as well as the effervescence of youth:

> each line
> of her tablet
> a different color,
> her young mind glowing
> like a rainbow

and the use of a curiously mundane yet novel object to summon associations of a different flavor of youth in a different era:

> just for fun
> plugging in
> my old lava lamp
> its curling colors
> as young as ever

The direct association of color with time in the final lines of that lava lamp tanka, the description of color as "young" to refer to literal brightness that hasn't faded in spite of age and plant a parallel—or contrast—to self-image, is intriguing and effective, the sort of simple and ingenuous but unique poetic device that prompts the reader who also writes tanka to wonder, "Why didn't that occur to me? Why didn't *I* ever think of that?" Interestingly, also, it follows another tanka that associates color with time in an unusual way—in this case, tim*ing* and naturally rhythmic pattern:

> on the cliff's edge
> three middle-aged women
> brandish paint brushes
> in time with the colors
> of waves on the rocks

Far more intriguing, though, is the author's dexterously varied and versatile incorporation of specific colors such as red, gold and grey to represent and communicate an expansive array of ideas, connotations and emotions. Red, especially, is startlingly and brilliantly adaptable in Rielly's figurative palette (possibly foreshadowed by the color of the flowers in the cover photo?). Reading this tanka for the first time is likely to induce a rapid seesaw of responses, from stark surprise, to grinning amusement, to appreciation of the poet's skill, to piqued and wondering curiosity:

> trying to attract
> hummingbirds I wonder whether
> a red light might work,
> but dismiss the thought
> for the sake of decorum

Here, what a red light alludes to is obvious, and its casual juxtaposition with something as benign and unsullied as hummingbirds generates an illustration of a flight of thought and spontaneous association of ideas just peculiar enough to be realistic.

In this way, this poem feels strangely and obliquely intimate, its perspective not overtly intrapersonal on the surface ("I wonder" may but does not *necessarily* signal internal monologue) but providing a lingering glance into an inner, unexpected and usually unseen fold in the routine churnings of a human imagination. That glance is a quality of several of Rielly's tanka collected in this book, albeit not as blatantly and not 'sneaking up on' the reader and jumping out in quite the same way as in this one. Take, for example, this poem on a brother's untimely passing:

> imagining again
> a brother dead longer
> than I have lived—
> what would he look like
> this morning at my table?

As in the hummingbird poem, the momentary destination of the narrator's wandering thoughts is oddly obvious in hindsight, yet unanticipated, and lies in a vaguely uncomfortable confluence of disparate domains that we may not even recognize the existence of until we find ourselves there. It is something many of us might think of in similar circumstances, but how many would admit it?

Returning to red:

> another blood test:
> the small red
> of my life
> flowing through a needle
> whose sting reassures me

This tanka, in a cluster of poems apparently about a hospital stay, raises another extant association with the color—here a magnified metonym, red as blood to red as life force—but twists it ever so slightly to render its manifestation unconventional, by contextualizing it in a situation of vulnerability. This is underlined by the preceding adjective "small," which simultaneously takes the red-as-life-force, red-as-vitality representation into a dimension (size) and assigns it an implication (vulnerability, precariousness) it typically isn't associated or co-occurring with, which facilitates the poem's effectiveness. Another tanka that references red blood and confronts vulnerability is an example of a contrasting technique that manipulates entrenched chromatic associations differently:

> the sink dotted
> with red from your cut
> finger, I scrub,
> thinking instead
> of your red hair

Instead of colliding it with a bizarrely unrelated image-situation, as the hummingbird tanka does, or subtly modifying the schema surrounding the association itself to suggest emotional undercurrents as seen in the blood test tanka, this poem derives its power from the nearly symmetrical superposition of one set of culturally-ingrained connotations over another to engender the contrast central to its meaning. Red hair is stereotypically associated with spirited, audacious personalities, which here is extended to resilience as the narrator focuses upon *that* image of a loved one—as lively—to dispel the more painful and distressing one in the first two lines—as wounded—and/or perhaps to inject a bit of humor (by implying that the injury may have been the indirect result somehow of relevant personality traits sometimes associated with red-haired people—e.g., stubbornness and intrepidity) in order to cope in the moment.

By adroitly wielding emblematic color associations in these differing but equally effective ways, Rielly manages to eke out a personal prismatic semiotics that is as distinctive and idiosyncratic as it is familiar. The reader is thereby drawn gently but definitely into his world, just beyond the surface of his sanctum where emotional articulation is buffered yet heartfelt and earnest. Rounding off his many red-shaded poems, of which only a sample is included in this review, is this tanka, one of several about his granddaughter in the final section:

> granddaughter's
> red circles
> in crayon
> revealing/masking
> her little world

Seemingly lacking any clear preexisting figurative or symbolic associations with the color red—or, potentially, putting forth a new one—this tanka leaves the reader wondering to what extent the red-based associations—and by extension all of the chromatic symbolism—in the numerous poems before it have served to both reveal and mask Rielly's inner "little world."

Something else Rielly does well in this collection is the candid and sentimental depiction of quotidian and homey scenes such that they remain interesting from a literary perspective rather than veering too far into monotonous or cloying territory, though not uniformly or perfectly. This tanka, most probably about interacting with trick-or-treating children, is one of the best examples of maintaining this poetic balance:

> writing tanka
> between visits
> from ghosts and goblins . . .
> the little witch tells me
> she's not a real one

What works in this poem is the 'surprise' shift following the third line (which really isn't, but like the adult on Halloween, the reader would be remiss not to kindly play along), and the ambiguity, temporary and contextually minimal yet still present, that sets it up. There is much to be learned from Rielly's related techniques throughout the collection (and in a few, unlike in the above, the ambiguity introduced via the language is never firmly resolved), as many tanka written in English grounded in the run-of-the-mill and routine elements of daily life suffer from a lack of plausible alternate possibilities for interpretation and consciously literary flair, thus failing to engage the reader and falling perhaps marginally short of self-justification for their existence as poetry. There are a handful of poems in *A Bed of Geraniums* that narrowly avoid this deficiency, but by and large the unmistakable imprint of intentional literary skill, in some form or another, prevails.

The one primary fault to be found with this collection lies in Rielly's copious use of punctuation, particularly commas. The trouble with commas in tanka is that they can easily and exclusively impose a sole specific 'flow' or pace of reading—which is frequently detrimental as the emphasis and hence meaning conveyed by the form relies heavily upon the reader's experience of that 'flow', as does, consequently, potential for interpretation. For example, the following tanka could have been considerably more effective had it been reworked to make sense without the commas:

> across the lawn
> between wings of the motel,
> stepping around
> fallen oranges, I walk
> into a lawn sprinkler

Although they do capture the harried disorientation of the narrator's walk, the effect of the commas is to emphasize the least-interesting part of the poem—namely the accident—by rushing it along to the end, where it's revealed. Motels are a connotatively loaded setting replete with interpretative possibilities—divorce? adultery? an adventurous road trip?—but here, the first comma nudges the reader ahead before those interpretations can be fully considered. The second comma is even worse in this respect, because of the accelerating motion that has already accumulated by that point in the poem, so any special significance carried by "fallen oranges" beyond their role as interchangeable obstacles is mainly lost. The whole structure seems contrived to make space for the pivot line, but its position squarely between the two commas encourages skimming too quickly over it as well.

On the other side of the punctuation coin, however, there is a tanka that uses a semicolon in the third line to pause the flow and extend the pivot in a masterful fashion:

> shooting star
> the night
> my brother died;
> it would be myth
> were it not true

In total, Rielly's scintillating application of chromatic symbolism, uncomplicated yet skillful use of other visual imagery, unassumingly restrained though candid sketches of features in his mental and emotional landscape, and general poetic aptitude make *A Bed of Geraniums* an exemplary and rewarding collection well worth reading.

The Flower in the Heart
Jenny Ward Angyal

Larry Hammer, translator. *Ice Melts in the Wind: The Seasonal Poems of the Kokinshu*. Tucson, Arizona: Cholla Bear Press, 2018. Perfect-bound paperback, 240 pages, 5.25 x 8 inches. ISBN 978-1-72882-641-7. $9.99.

> Yet if not to you,
> then to whom might I show it?
> The flowering plum!
> Only the knowing can know
> both its color and its scent.
> —*Ki no Tomonori*

"Only the knowing can know . . ." What are we to make of this cryptic statement? Translator Larry Hammer tells us that, in Japanese esthetics, to know the color of a thing is to know only its superficial beauty, while to know its scent is to grasp its true nature.

The poems in *Ice Melts in the Wind* and in Hammer's translation that is the subject of the following review—tanka penned over a thousand years ago—testify to both the beautiful surface of the world and to its true nature as transient, ever-changing, and ungraspable.

The *Kokinshu*, compiled around 905 C.E., was the first imperially commissioned anthology of poetry written in Japanese. It comprised over a thousand poems organized in six books of seasonal poems and five books of love poems, plus some smaller miscellaneous themes. The vast majority are what we now call tanka. *Ice Melts in the Wind* is a new translation of the six books of seasonal poems: 342 tanka arranged according to the progression of the seasons. Each poem is presented in English along with a transliteration of the original Japanese text.

Translator Larry Hammer also provides a useful introduction and extensive commentary on the poems, including context and background as well as discussion of possible alternative translations and the challenges of translating between such vastly different cultures and languages. Insofar as possible, he has chosen to render the poems in lines of 5/7/5/7/7 syllables, notwithstanding the oft-noted differences between Japanese sound units and English-language syllables. The book also includes a list of sources and an index to the poets, with brief notes on their lives.

The first two books are devoted to spring, beginning in late winter:

> In the valley wind
> the river ice is melting,
> and in every crack
> the little waves that spurt out—
> the first flowers of springtime?
> —*Minamoto no Masazumi*

The charming confusion of ice or snow with flowers is a common trope at this season, and one that recurs at the end of the year. As the season progresses, cherry blossoms arrive:

> These cherries must bloom
> with the same scent and color
> as in days gone by,
> and indeed what changes is
> people who age with the years.
> —*Ki no Tomonori*

The scent and color of the blossoms—both their essence and their beauty—remain the same year after year, in poignant contrast with the brevity of non-returning human lives. In the second book of spring poems, the fading of those same blossoms provides yet another reminder of mortality:

> How they resemble
> our cicada-shell world!
> —even while we watch
> the flowering cherries bloom,
> they're already scattering.
> —*Author unknown*

The translator explains that "like a cicada shell" is a stock epithet for the world, referring to the Buddhist idea that human existence is as empty and ephemeral as the molted casing of a cicada nymph.

Summer, in book three, brings the cuckoo:

> O cuckoo who sings
> in the summertime mountains,
> if you have a heart,
> do not make me hear your voice—
> I already feel so much.
> —*Author unknown*

The cuckoo's song as an occasion for melancholy is a common trope borrowed from Chinese poetry, and the cuckoo occurs in 28 of the 34 poems of summer. The repetition of images is not unique to summer—bush warblers, plum blossoms and cherry blossoms abound in spring, while autumn is well-stocked with wild geese, crickets and chrysanthemums. The poems may therefore seem repetitious to Western readers who prize originality; but this is a different esthetic, one that values the ability to reference familiar poems and tropes while giving them a slightly novel twist.

Take, for example, this tanka from the first of the two books of autumn poems:

> The approaching boats
> raising their voices with their sails
> in the autumn wind—
> these are in fact the wild geese
> crossing the gates of heaven
> —*Fujiwara no Sugane*

In his commentary on this poem, Larry Hammer tells us that, while comparing sails to wings is common everywhere, and comparing the honking of geese to the creak of oars was traditional in Chinese poetry, having the boats "raising their voices" under sail seems to be Sugane's original touch—the sort of variation prized in *Kokinshu* poetics.

Autumn, of course, lends itself to the theme of impermanence:

> Let's pluck and wear you,
> O chrysanthemum flower,
> while there's still dew—
> that never-aging autumn
> must then abide forever.
> —*Ki no Tomonori*

The vain hope of "abiding forever" is encouraged by Chinese folklore, which promised that drinking the dew from a chrysanthemum could slow aging, or perhaps even confer immortality. But autumn always progresses toward winter:

> The warp of frost and
> weft of dew must be fragile.
> The very moment
> the brocade of the mountains
> weaves itself, it comes apart.
> —*Fujiwara no Sekio*

This exquisite image of beauty and transience is slightly marred by the translator's awkward line breaks, especially in the upper verse. I do not read Japanese and cannot comment on the original poem, but the English-language tanka poet in me itches to rework these (and other) lovely lines for a smoother read, discarding the artificial constraint of 5/7/5/7/7.

Winter, like summer, is a single, short book. Lacking the day-by-day changes so evident in spring and autumn, summer and winter seem less apt to inspire the poignant poems of transience. In winter we return, as in early spring, to the trope of snow as flowers, which here serves as a metaphor for hope in dark times:

> Although it's winter,
> with this scattering of flowers
> come down from the sky—
> might it be that it's springtime
> away beyond the clouds?
> —*Kiyowara no Fukayabu*

The book concludes with a few poems on the New Year:

> Every single time
> the always-renewing year
>   comes to an end,
> both the snow and my body
> continue to ever fall.
> —*Ariwara no Motokata*

And we come full circle—the ever-repeating cycle of the seasons standing in poignant contrast to the one-way trajectory of human life.

Ono no Komachi's Dreams
Jenny Ward Angyal

Larry Hammer, translator. *These Things Called Dreams: The Poems of Ono no Komachi*. Tucson, Arizona: Cholla Bear Press, 2019. Perfect-bound paperback, 52 pages, 6 x 9 inches. ISBN 978-1-79057-762-0. $9.99.

The seasons of the year, the seasons of the human heart—these are the two great themes of the *Kokinshu*. Larry Hammer has yet to translate its five books of love poetry, but in *These Things Called Dreams* he offers 22 poems by Ono no Komachi, 18 of which appear in the *Kokinshu*, and most of which are love poems.

Little is known about Ono no Komachi, who probably lived and wrote in the mid-800s. She is considered one of the "Six Poetic Sages" of the early Heian period. In addition to the 22 poems that can with certainty be attributed to Komachi, *These Things Called Dreams* also includes three poems by other poets with whom she wrote responsively.

This is a very beautiful little book, with 22 illustrations, most of them full-page and most of them in color. These *kasen-e*—imagined portraits of famous poets, often paired with a particular poem—belong to a genre dating back to the 12th century, although these portraits of Komachi were mostly rendered in the 18th and 19th centuries. Larry Hammer provides notes about the context of each picture, many of which illustrate charming legends about the life of Komachi.

Her poems express love, longing, and sorrow, often making use of striking images:

> But doesn't he know
> he can't see me through the seaweed
>   of my sorrow's shores—
> this fisherman who comes here
> ceaselessly on weary legs?

Is the visitor perhaps "fishing" for the esteem of this famous and fickle beauty, who is hidden by the "seaweed of her sorrow's shores," perhaps still grieving the loss of another lover?

> Those times when I long
> for you so very keenly,
>   I wear through the night
> dark as leopard-lily seeds
> my sleeping robes inside out.

According to folklore, sleeping with your nightclothes inside-out allows you to dream of the object of your desire. The translator says that "dark as leopard-lily seeds" is a stock epithet for "night," but it is certainly a beautiful one!

Even in love—or especially in love?—the awareness of impermanence, loss and change is pervasive:

> So it's over now—
> my body falls into age
>   with the autumn rains,
> and even your words like leaves
> have faded and scattered.

Does the poet feel old because her lover's attentions have "faded," or has he lost interest because she has indeed "fallen into age"? Either way, the poem expresses the knowledge that ultimately all things fade and scatter "with the autumn rains." This is the poignant and perennial insight given voice in these two books of thousand-year-old poems, which Larry Hammer has made accessible to the modern, Western reader.

> So indeed it is:
> that which changes and fades,
>   its colors unseen,
> is the flower in the heart
> of a man inside the world.

Chrysanthemums Soar
Jenny Ward Angyal

Vasile Moldovan. *Between Sky and Earth: Tanka Poems*. Bucharest: Romanian Writers' Society Publishing House, 2019. Perfect-bound paperback, 80 pages, 5 x 7.5 inches, ISBN 978-606-8412-64-1. Available from the author at vasilemoldovan1949@gmail.com.

> In the palm
> of the blind beggar
> a gift from the sky
> came suddenly —
> first snowflake

A gift from the sky falls to earth, into the hand of a blind beggar. The tanka can be read literally and also as metaphor — perhaps we are all in some sense blind beggars in need of such unexpected grace. *Between Sky and Earth* is the second volume of tanka by Romanian poet Vasile Moldovan; his first, *After the Tempest*, appeared in 2013. *Between Sky and Earth* is aptly named. Ten themed sections, comprising 138 tanka in Romanian and in English translations by the poet, explore themes of heaven and earth: dreams and religion, poetry and time, love and family, nature's beauty and the world's pain.

Vasile Moldovan co-edited *Atlas Poetica*'s first-ever special feature, "25 Romanian Tanka Poets, in Romanian and English," published in 2010. It included an interesting history of tanka in Romania, where the form evidently continues to thrive; a second Romanian Special Feature went online four years later. That tanka are being written in so many different languages across the globe testifies to the power of these small songs, and Vasile Moldovan's poems are no exception.

> A poetry
> without words
> says so much . . .
> in a deep silence
> I hear my heartbeats

Tanka is a poetry of few words, and much of its power resides in what is not said. Surely that is part of its broad international appeal; its ability to cross borders and connect people of different cultures and languages, as in this bilingual volume.

Romania is a nation with a complex history and many international borders. In the book's title section, "Between Earth and Sky," several poems explore the illusory nature of the borders that too often seem to separate earth from sky and people from each other.

> Birds and butterflies
> flying both sides
> of the borderline
> without any charge and
> without a passport

Such freedom to transcend borders is an ideal the human species has yet to attain, and the poet does not shy away from confronting the harsher realities that divide us:

> Waiting for news
> from the Middle East . . .
> four soldiers
> pull out from the plane
> another coffin of zinc

Resonating throughout the book is the poet's longing for human beings to understand and implement a different way of being in this world, a way more attuned to the ways of nature—or, perhaps, of heaven:

> Lying in the grass
> I listen to the voice of flowers—
> how much I wish
> also my fellows
> to understand it

Unfortunately, I know no Romanian, so I cannot judge the quality of language in the original tanka. Although the English translations are sometimes marred by awkwardness, as in the last lines of the poem above, the poet's earnest and ardent heartbeat can be clearly heard in this poetry of few words carefully chosen.

Readers will be grateful that Vasile Moldovan has taken the trouble to render into English, for the benefit of the wider tanka community, his beautiful and uplifting insights.

> Prayer
> in the flower garden—
> I feel again how
> chrysanthemums soar
> toward heaven

Three Tanka Books for Children
Michael Dylan Welch

Tony Medina et al. *Thirteen Ways of Looking at a Black Boy.* Oklahoma City, Oklahoma: Penny Candy Books, 2018. 978-0-9987999-4-0, hardback, 40 pages.

Robert Paul Weston, illustrated by Misa Saburi. *Sakura's Cherry Blossoms.* Toronto, Ontario: Tundra Books, 2018. 978-1-101-91874-6, hardback, 40 pages.

Nikki Grimes. *Garvey's Choice.* Honesdale, Pennsylvania: Wordsong, 2016. 978-1-62979-740-3, hardback, 108 pages.

It's been common for decades for children's books to feature haiku. Less common are children's books of tanka, but it seems that such books have enjoyed an uptick in numbers in recent years. Two examples published in 2018 are Tony Medina's *Thirteen Ways of Looking at a Black Boy*, and Robert Paul Weston's *Sakura's Cherry Blossoms*. However, neither book seems sufficiently aware of literary approaches to tanka, although Medina's book, in terms of tanka, is the more successful of the two. In terms of being children's books, both publications are beautifully illustrated and successful for the audiences they intend to reach. A third book featuring tanka, intended for older youth, is *Garvey's Choice* by Nikki Grimes, published in 2016. But trouble lies afoot in this book too, even if just from the perspective of adult readers.

Let me start with Medina's book. Penny Candy Books also recently published Sydell Rosenberg's *H Is for Haiku*, and readers might well hope that the press will continue to support Japanese poetry forms. The title of Medina's *Thirteen Ways* immediately brings to mind the Wallace Stevens poem, "Thirteen Ways of Looking at a Blackbird," with the twist of focusing on African American culture. Notes at the end of the book mention other books that have alluded to Stevens' poem. Additional notes assume that tanka is merely 5-7-5-

7-7 syllables, a pattern that is evidenced in the poems themselves, as if that's all there is to it, but the explanation does at least add that the poem's images should *show* ideas rather than explain them. Most important in the notes is the mention of place in poetry, and how these poems focus on Anacostia, an historically black neighborhood in the southeast section of Washington, D.C. Each poem depicts a person or place in the neighborhood or presents a more universal image. Each poem, which is titled (tanka are usually not titled), is also presented with extraordinary artwork by thirteen African American artists and as such is a remarkable work of collaboration. Here's the book's opening poem, titled "Anacostia Angels" (6):

> Fly bow tie like wings
>   Brown eyes of a brown angel
> His kool-aid smile sings
>   Mama's little butterfly
> Daddy's dimple grin so wide

Such a poem may serve the book's purpose but would not be likely to be accepted for any of the leading tanka journals publishing in English. The book's extensive bios for the poet and each of the thirteen artists seem more in service to the contributors than to young readers (in other words, I doubt children would read them), but they provide a context for adults that honors the ethnic background common to each contributor. The poems are the main attraction, of course (with the artwork), and the poems show different black boys in unique and celebratory ways—depicting not just children but the black "boys" of all ages that pepper this particular neighborhood, one that thereby represents any ethnic neighborhood in America. It's a book of recognition and validation, which is more important than whether it uses tanka or not. As such, this book may appeal to the widest range of readers of three books I explore here and may offer wider benefits to classroom use and to families and libraries.

Robert Paul Weston's *Sakura's Cherry Blossoms*, illustrated sumptuously by Misa Saburi, is a more traditional children's book, in contrast with Medina's book. This is an immigration story, dealing with cultural differences that come to be a source of joy instead of stress and loss. The story is told using "tanka," counted out in 5-7-5-7-7 syllables, with a blank line after the first three lines, a presentation choice that might invoke renku or renga for those who are familiar with this Japanese linked-verse form that grew out of waka and is intertwined with the history of tanka—and later, haiku. Here's the book's opening verse, which introduces the story's title character, a little girl named Sakura (4):

> Sakura loved spring,
> her favorite time of year.
> This made perfect sense.
>
> Her name means cherry blossom,
> trees that only bloom in spring.

Remaining verses unfold in a similarly explanatory and narrative manner. They demonstrate little feeling for the established aesthetics and techniques of tanka poetry as a literary art, but they do paint a pleasing story of the girl remembering her Japanese grandmother, with whom she went to view cherry blossoms. Sakura has just moved to America because of her father's new job. She has to learn a new language (where *neko* becomes *cat*), and that autumn she has trouble fitting in at her new school. She is also too shy to talk with Luke, the boy who lives next door. But he eventually talks with her, and they become friends through a love of astronomy. Sakura says, "Flowers are like stars," and that they blossom and sparkle, and then "they fade, so we treasure them / because one day they vanish" (19). This thought foreshadows the girl's relationship with her beloved grandmother. Sakura and her family soon have to go back to Japan to visit the girl's dying grandmother, who had told her that seeing the blossoms "is always finest with friends" (9). Sakura is still sad when she returns to America in the winter. But Luke has a surprise for her, because it is almost springtime. This verse explains what happens next (36):

The entire city
burst to life, flowers blooming
on every corner.

By the river, both its shores
blazed bright with cherry blossoms!

Sakura's family and Luke's family enjoy the blossoms together and Sakura learns for herself how her grandmother was right, that "watching cherry blossoms bloom / is always finest with friends" (39), giving the book a pleasing sense of closure. It's a beautiful and heartwarming story, and a recommended book for young children dealing with the loss of a grandparent or other relative (or even a pet), or perhaps just facing the challenge of moving to a new home. It's also a possible way to introduce tanka to young readers, but some tanka writers may feel that it does a disservice to tanka by presuming that all one needs to do is count 5-7-5-7-7 syllables, even though English syllables are not equivalent to the sounds counted in Japanese tanka. It's a shame, even for the youngest of readers, that tanka is reduced to the following "explanation" at the end of the book (40), with no hint of a deeper understanding, and that no demonstration of tanka as a literary art appears in the poems themselves:

I am a tanka
a poem with five short lines
count my syllables

you will know I am finished
when you get to thirty-one

One might respond that this is a possible starting point for young readers—as with haiku, you can at least begin to explore tanka by counting syllables. However, when this counting of syllables is based on a fundamental misunderstanding of the differences between the two languages, why give children such misinformation, and not say anything about more important targets? Even young children could handle a little bit more, and certainly deserve more accuracy (yet I recognize that the author is a victim of these misunderstandings too). This misinformation is perhaps more injurious to young readers because of how much more impressionable they are at that age. *Sakura's Cherry Blossoms* is such a beautiful story, with lovely illustrations, but like so many tanka books for children (and more commonly, haiku books) it perpetuates a misunderstanding of the genre. While the vast majority of readers won't care to the degree that established tanka poets will, the problem remains that children (and their unsuspecting parents) will become indoctrinated with misleading information.

An earlier tanka book for children, one with similar issues, is *Garvey's Choice* by Nikki Grimes, published in 2016, aimed at an older audience than the preceding two picture books. It's an example of the trend of young adult verse novels, where a story is told in poetic stanzas, in this case using "tanka." The story's main character, Garvey, is about twelve years old, and readers see through the window of the book's poems into his middle-school world. But why tanka, and what does the author think it to be? In a note of explanation at the end, Grimes says she chose to use the 5-7-5-7-7 syllabic form, but adds that "Not every American poet follows a syllable count for tanka poems, but I think of a syllable count like a puzzle. Each word is a puzzle piece, and I like figuring out which words fit best" (107). Of course, as with haiku, the "puzzle" of tanka has greater challenges than merely counting syllables, and we see almost no attempt in these poems to meet those more significant challenges (the same was true in her prior book of haiku for children, *A Pocketful of Poems*, a gorgeous publication from Clarion Books in 2001). The author does say she tried to give each tanka a "mood," but acknowledges that her focus "is more centered on telling a story" (107). Indeed, the book presents prose that is arbitrarily broken into verses of 5-7-5-7-7 syllables. Although the line breaks are usually artfully done, that's not always the case, and most of the poems cannot work alone as independent poems, especially so in the following middle verse of three under the heading of "Saturday

Play" (21; Angela is Garvey's sister) and the third verse of four from "It's Manny Now" (61):

> and it goes like this:
> Dad juggles his ball like a
> hot potato, asks,
> "Who's up for running passes?"
> Angela always rises.

> are you staring at?"
> "Nothing. I've just never seen
> a sandwich like that."
> "*Mmm*," Manny hums between bites.
> "You don't know what you're missing.

The book's narrative succeeds on its own inspirational and timely terms, but readers will be hard-pressed to find justification for the text's presentation in "tanka" form. Verse novels have been a recent trend in children's literature, but here the presumed form for tanka seems incidental and arbitrary to the plot and characters (and the same issue would be true if another form of poetry had been used—many verse novels seem similarly gimmicky). The verses make no attempt to explore tanka aesthetics or most strategies commonly used by tanka poets—they just redistribute bits of prose as syllable countings (although not without care). The sets of "tanka" do give the book pacing, however, and the titles are not so much titles of individual poems as they are of "sequences" (each developing the plot or the characters in some way), even when many of the book's sequences have just one poem. Here is the book's title sequence, "Garvey's Choice," presenting the moment when Garvey acts on his decision to join his school's chorus at an audition (54):

Ignoring my nerves,
I march into the classroom,
squeak out why I've come.
Feeling numb, I take a breath,
tickle that first note, then soar.

My voice skips octaves
like a smooth stone on a lake.
That's when they tell me.
"Well, class," says the director,
"Guess we found our new tenor."

As mentioned, the book is far more successful as a story than as tanka, and on this level *Garvey's Choice* comes well recommended. Garvey is pressured by his dad to play sports, but that isn't what the boy wants to do, and Garvey doesn't understand why his dad wants to do sports together (we learn later that the dad is hoping to bond with his son, rather than just trying to promote a sport or being more "macho"). Garvey is also bullied at school, but thanks to good friendships he learns to stand up for himself, ignoring teasers and name-callers. Garvey joins the school chorus because he loves music, and through music he builds a stronger identity. Perhaps his interest in music is the thinnest possible connection to tanka, as if tanka is thereby a musical way of telling the story, but that seems to be the closest we come to understanding why tanka was used for *this* story. Garvey's friends, Joe and Manny, "get" him and understand his love of singing and other interests, and his lack of interest in football and basketball. Garvey also struggles with his weight, but starts jogging, inspired by his friends. He finally connects with his dad when his dad rejoins the old band he was in, as a singer—inspired by his son's choice to join the school chorus. This is a book about self-esteem and ultimately identity, presenting issues that any middle-schooler might face, including relationships with parents. Here's how the book ends, with a single poem under the heading of "Summer Duet":

Dad's old band tunes up
at our house on Saturdays.
You should hear how his
bluesy bass rhythms rock my
high-tenor melodies—sweet!

We should all wish for positive endings like this, whether "tanka" is used to get there or not. Tanka poets may well find themselves distracted by the usurpation of tanka in this manner, but if they can look past that, they will find a beautifully written story. This is a characteristic that all three of these books share in common, and we might hope for a more informed sort of tanka to find its way into future children's books, but for now we can celebrate at least small steps in the direction of more and more tanka appearing among books of poetry for children.

News and Announcements

Congratulations to all the winners and honorable mentions of The 2019 San Francisco International Competition for Haiku, Senryu and Tanka!

FIRST PLACE

our long conversation
about divorcing
we part company
soundlessly
in falling snow

Pamela A. Babusci, Rochester, NY

This conversation in falling snow provides a sense of acceptance, despite the cold—a coldness that seems figurative as well as literal. The word "soundlessly" makes this poem click into place, connecting the nature of the relationship with the natural elements. What is possibly beautiful in nature is perhaps not so beautiful in the relationship. More importantly, we can see that the relationship has gone cold, and we get the feeling that this parting of company is not just at that moment but permanently. The poem offers a bittersweet sadness with the fitting image of falling snow. The soundlessness cements that acceptance, too, which provides a hint of positiveness.

—*Michael Dylan Welch, tanka judge*

TANKA SECOND PLACE

in my dream
Mother is still alive—
I fall back to sleep
to finish our stroll
in the summer garden

Margaret Chula, Portland, OR

An unspoken grief and a feeling of loss serve as an undercurrent to this buoyant poem. The poet is remembering Mother in happier times, and the dream enables the poet to linger with those memories. I find it fitting, too, that this is a summer garden, when nature is at its prime, and the dream is surely of a time when the mother was in her prime as well, perhaps also being a gardener herself. The poem's conversation and companionship, and ultimately the love that binds these two people together, make this an inviting poem, but not without a mix of sadder feelings also.

TANKA THIRD PLACE

some scars lie deeper
than can ever be seen . . .
the other mourners
mistake my tears for grief
instead of joy

Tracy Davidson, Warwickshire, UK

TANKA HONORABLE MENTIONS

a cumulous cloud
dissipating . . .
would anyone
notice
if I disappeared

Susan Burch, Hagerstown, MD

the coiled tips
of fiddlehead ferns
remind me
that every forest knows
how to make music

Debbie Strange, Winnipeg, Manitoba, Canada

sewing a button
onto his shirt—
at least this
I know how
to fix

Susan Burch, Hagerstown, MD

~ ~ ~ ~

The winners of the 2020 Fujisan Tanka Grand Prix English Tanka Department contest were recently announced. Congratulations to our TSA member, for winning first place!

> seen from the snow-cap
> the vast plains below
> in every direction
> the world unfolds
> a map of our planet

Beatrice Yell, Australia

Honorable mentions include several TSA members, namely, Michael H. Lester, Maryalicia Post, Edward J. Rielly, Autumn Noelle Hall, Michael McClintock, Genie Nakano, Susan Mary Wade, Bob Lucky, Julie Bloss Kelsey, and Kath Abela Wilson. You can find the full details here: http://fujisantaisho.com/index_english.html

~ ~ ~ ~

Amanda DCosta, David Terelinck, and Christine L. Villa would like to thank all those who sent their entries and donations to Climate Change: The Burning Issue, a tanka competition and fundraiser for koala rescue and rehabilitation following the recent Australian bushfire disaster. The competition will be blind judged by David Terelinck. Results will be announced no later than April 30, 2020. In the second half of 2020, an anthology of the best tanka will be published by Christine L. Villa under the imprint Velvet Dusk Publishing in collaboration with Mandy's Pages, and will be available for purchase online. For full details, visit www.mandys-pages.com.

we trundle
to the rusty school bus
you hold
my hand through snowdrifts
deeper than summer dreams

words/image©QStrange

Index of Contributors

Submission Guidelines

Submissions to *Ribbons*, the Tanka Society of America's journal, are open to TSA members and non-members alike.

Ribbons submission deadlines are in-hand no later than

April 30: Spring/Summer Issue
August 31: Fall Issue
December 31: Winter Issue

The *Ribbons* editors will respond to all submissions within one month of the submission deadline.

Your submissions must not be under consideration elsewhere, submitted to any contest, or previously published anywhere at any time, including online; however, tanka posted to online workshop lists or on Facebook are permissible. All rights revert to authors upon publication, except that the TSA reserves the right to reprint content from its publications on TSA social media sites and its website.

Ribbons seeks fresh material of the highest standard to present to our readers. Any tanka with a sensibility that distinguishes the form will be considered. Therefore, we welcome different syllable counts, varying individual styles and techniques, and are open to diverse yet appropriate subject material. We also welcome essays that offer fresh insights and information.

Tanka: You are welcome to submit *either* up to ten original, unpublished tanka *or* two tanka sequences (not more than six links) for each issue, plus essays, interviews, news, and announcements. Submissions by email are preferred. Submit to clvribbons@gmail.com with the subject heading "*Ribbons* Submissions." You can also submit by postal mail:

Christine L. Villa, *Ribbons* Editor
5040 Jackson St., #86, North Highlands, CA 95660

Tanka Prose: Send one tanka prose piece to our tanka prose editor, Susan Weaver, at tankaproseribbons@gmail.com. Please put "*Ribbons* Submission" in the subject line. While submissions by email are preferred, you may also submit tanka prose by postal mail:

Susan Weaver, *Ribbons* Tanka Prose Editor
127 N. 10th Street, Allentown, PA 18102

Prose count should not exceed 300 words. Number of tanka is "unlimited" (within reason and when in service to the whole). Please include a creative title.

Regarding frequency of submission, tanka prose writers whose work is accepted are asked to hold off from contributing tanka prose again for at least one submission period after publication. This policy gives more tanka prose poets an opportunity to share their work and also lets us represent the many ways tanka prose is being written today.

Book Reviews: Please send books to review to our book review editor, Tamara K. Walker, by postal mail:

Tamara K. Walker, *Ribbons* Book Review Editor
6127 W. Elmhurst Drive, Littleton, CO 80128

Each tanka related book received will be acknowledged by title, author, and ordering information, with a sentence or two about the book. One or more books will be selected for full review. If you wish to query the book reviewer by mail first: heliotropicink@gmail.com.

Note: These submission guidelines do not apply to submissions to the Tanka Café column (open to TSA members only). For Tanka Café guidelines, see a current issue of *Ribbons* or the TSA website. Send Tanka Café submissions to Michael McClintock at MchlMcClintock@aol.com with Tanka Café as the subject heading or by postal mail to: Michael McClintock, 183 N. Bush Avenue, Clovis, CA 93619.